# A EXTRA KNOT

## A Different World War
### (PART I)

# HUGH LUPUS

APS BOOKS

An Extra Knot (Part I) ©2019 APS Publications
All rights reserved.

HMS Hood Photograph Allan C Green/Restoration Adam Cuerdon

A catalogue record for this book is available from the British Library

ISBN 978-1-78996-022-8

APS Publications,
4 Oakleigh Road,
Stourbridge,
West Midlands,
DY8 2JX

www.andrewsparke.com

To my wife whose patience passeth all understanding.

# INTRODUCTION

Look down.

Look down this May morning in 1941.

Look down on grey cold waves.

Look down as giant ships manoeuvre and throw high explosives at each other.

Watch as great founts of water erupt around one of the giants as she strides through the ocean, eager to meet her foes.

Already she has been wounded, but the blow has not dampened her ardour as she fires back.

Look down now as a towering explosion looms over the eager ship.

A blow, a mortal blow has struck her.

Already one part of the ship has disappeared, but her bow, though standing vertically in the water is still afloat.

The ship, what little remains of her will surely take no further part in the battle.

But stay now.

Stay and watch a miracle.

The ship begins to slip beneath the waves, but before it does, it fires at the enemy. Even in its death throes the ship has found the energy for a last desperate act.

Feel now.

Feel the ship and know.

Know that ships have souls.

Souls made up of the thoughts and senses of every man who built them and every sailor who had ever voyaged with them.

Feel.

Feel the ships dying emotions.

There is fury.

A baffled, surprised fury that she has been beaten so swiftly.

Regret.

Regret that she has failed to protect her men, men she had loved and cherished.

Agony.

Agony as the pain of her death begins to filter through.

Sorrow.

Sorrow that there would be no more tomorrows.

But overlaying all those sensations is one overarching emotion.

Pride.

Pride over what she had been, what she had represented and what she still was.

She was a fighting ship and her pride dictated that she would go down still fighting, still hurling death at her enemy.

And so on a grey Atlantic morning H.M.S Hood, the pride of a navy supreme dies.

But ask.

Ask if that pride could be given a second chance.

Ask if there is a different path to take.

Watch.

Watch as time runs backwards.

Watch as the Hood rises out of the water and begins to heal herself.

The awful explosion is sucked back into the bowels of the ship and she begins to retreat from her enemies who seem equally anxious to avoid contact with her.

Watch as time runs and runs.

Eating through the months.

Eating through the years.

Seek.

Seek the chance to deflect time's arrow and avert disaster.

And find it.

To save the Hood.

To give the world a war.

A different war.

# COLLISION

In the year 1935 Spain was on the verge of tearing itself apart.

Out here on the ocean there was an unusual calm, but on the land there was confusion and unrest. Fathers were dividing against sons, sisters against mothers. Each and every side was convinced that it, and it alone knew of the one true path.

Normally civil unrest, even a European civil war would be only of academic interest to the Royal Navy. The sort of thing that would be read of in the mess in week old editions of The Times...after the cricket scores of course.

But this time it was different, this time there were outside players with their own agendas. Players who would use the Spanish people's agony as a testing ground not only for new weapons and techniques but also the resolve of other nations.

Which is why some of the Royal Navy's capital ships along with numerous smaller units had left Gibraltar and were now performing graceful and it was hoped warlike exercises off the Spanish coast.

Many of those aboard the ships that day believed that as a training exercise the sortie was an acceptable use of time, but as a diplomatic display it was barely better than doing nothing. And doing nothing seemed to be the semi-official policy of many nations.

That though was not the concern of the ships. Today the Battlecruisers Renown and Hood would separate, each taking a complement of smaller ships with them. Then throughout the day each group would engage the other acting the part of a determined, skilful enemy.

The admiral's orders were to make things as difficult for the gunnery officers as possible. Speed and course would be altered without notice, everything that could be done to make gun laying difficult would be done. In war it was unlikely that the enemy would have the courtesy to walk up to the Navy's guns in a straight line, so it was better to practice now in peace, than suffer later in battle.

And so the morning went, ships appeared over the horizon, dodged and feinted like aquatic matadors, gun layers cursed and sweated seeking desperately to keep opposing ships constantly within range and on target. Captains trembled hoping that any ship but theirs would fail today.

Until it ended.

The admiral was satisfied that his fleet was a little sharper and the world was reminded that the Royal Navy had a long reach. The signal was made for one last manoeuvre, then Hood and Renown would then race for home and the bars and bordellos of Gibraltar. The day had been cold but calm, the exercise had gone well. All together a good mornings work for the Royal Navy.

Or so it would seem

Midshipman Pulver had long heeded the advice that junior officers were equipped with two ears and one mouth, and therefore it would be best if he did twice as much listening as speaking and it would be far better still if he never spoke at all. So during his time in the engine room he did his very best to remain inconspicuous while gathering the maximum information.

The Hood's chief engineer was a gruff man, old enough to be Pulver's father, who had greeted him with a barely concealed exasperation and ordered Pulver to study the engine room manuals.

Pulver, being the boy that he was, did not see this as an attempt to stop him from getting under the feet of the engine room crew which it undoubtedly was, but as an opportunity to gain valuable information. So he studied the manuals until he knew them backwards and forwards.

When rather furtively he began to patrol the walkways of the engine rooms seeking to link his newly acquired knowledge with physical reality it was as if the books had come to life. Each dial, each gauge and every steam line or whirling shaft had its counterpoint on the pages that Pulver had memorised. To his mind they were twins, differing only in minor details.

Today's patrol was no different. He walked past machinery nodding to them as if they were old friends and occasionally reaching out to touch them reassuringly. It was only when he walked past a bank of gauges that his patrol halted.

Being a cautious boy and remembering the advice given him he thought very hard before acting. Finally, taking his courage in both hands and with feet dragging he walked up to the chief engineer and addressed the man's back.

'Excuse me sir.'

The man whirled round obviously annoyed at being interrupted.

'Yes, what is it?'

Pulver recoiled from the man's anger but realised that he was in too deep now to withdraw.

'Excuse me sir but weren't we ordered to make revolutions for twelve knots?'

The engineer raised his eyebrows to heaven.

'Midshipman and their damn fool questions', he thought, 'And to think that the future of the Navy depended on boys like this!' Still this particular specimen had been less trouble than most so he swallowed his exasperation and replied as calmly as a busy man who had been interrupted could.

'Yes Mr. Pulver twelve knots was the last order and it hasn't changed.'

Pulver took a deep breath and spoke the sentence that he hoped would not blight his career before it had truly begun.

'But I've just walked past the master discovery board and the pressure to the turbines isn't enough to give us twelve knots.'

He looked at the engineer's face as it grew redder and redder until Pulver was sure that the man was about to explode. Instead there was a sort of strangled scream which died before it could mature and blast the midshipman into eternity.

The stillborn scream mutated into words and action. Pulver immediately realised that the chief engineer may have been an old man, but old or not his muscles were anything but decrepit. The midshipman's elbow was held in a grip of steel and a voice all the more dangerous because of its suppressed anger hissed in his ear.

'Nonsense boy I checked those gauges not twenty minutes ago and everything was fine.'

His grip increased and rivers of pain began to run up and down Pulver's arm.

'If this is some sort of joke I'll have you up on report by the end of the watch, and before the Captain before the day ends. Come with me.'

Pulver had no choice as the grip on his elbow had not relaxed, and together man and boy marched towards the bank of dials that told just how much steam was delivered to the great turbines that drove the long spinning drive shafts. Only then was the grip released but the midshipman denied his body's urgent request to rub the circulation back into his injured arm. Instead he watched fascinated as the engineer tapped gauges and muttered arcane formulas to himself. After what seemed an age he came to a decision and turned to a still nervous Pulver.

'Boy, go down to the reduction gears and tell me the readings. I want to know what each shaft is doing.'

Pulver turned to run, but the hand reached out again, this time much gentler.

'Walk boy, don't run. Officers never run it sets a bad example, but quick as you can.'

It took only minutes for Pulver to walk through into the other two engine rooms and quickly note down the readings from the turning shafts but when he reported back the picture was clear. There was insufficient power going to every shaft. The Hood was moving through the water approximately one knot below that ordered by the bridge.

Muttering curses the chief ordered each engine room to open the great wheels which held the steam captive. Just a small fraction more of the steams great power was released to the turbines but gradually the battle cruiser began to move through the water a little faster.

A little faster, imperceptibly ,fractionally faster.

But enough.

Just enough.

Neither the chief engineer, Pulver, nor any one of the Hood's crew ever knew that they had been tricked by their own instruments. They never knew that all their gauges had been contaminated by debris, flowing past a faulty filter, never knew that every gauge under read by just a small amount. They never knew that from the moment they gave the turbines a fraction more steam they condemned several of fellow crew members to death. They never knew that from that moment their world, their very lives began to diverge from what was into what would be.


The chief engineer had unbent just a little and Pulver realised just what a high honour he was receiving as he was personally taken around the cavernous engine rooms by the great man himself.

Standing in the aft engine room watching the starboard inner drive shaft rotate at what they now believed to be at the correct rate he knew that only a few yards from him kept at bay only by the ships structure and twelve inches of armour plate lay the sea, and behind him four, twenty-ton propellers pushed the Hood's bulk through the water.

'Enough energy to power a small-town Mr Pulver, the Captain may give the orders but without us down here he may as well be shouting into the wind. Once Renown and her group have re-joined us the Captain has promised us a high-speed run back to Gibraltar.'

Pulver had never seen his ship perform at high speed before and the concept intrigued him.

'When will Renown join us sir?'

The engineer looked at his watch.

'Any moment now.'

He paused, embarrassed a little by his earlier outburst. Midshipmen were generally a bloody nuisance but this one showed that he had a good eye. Maybe something could be made of him.

'You did well today Mr Pulver. Very well, it wasn't an easy thing to spot but you did…well done.'

Now it was Pulver's turn to have a red face. Praise even for a job well done had not been a big part of his life so far. The Navy seemed to assume that excellence in any task was completely normal and only to be expected. He tried not to let his discomfort show.

'Thank you Mr Roberts.'

He received a rare, though wintery smile in return.

'Aye we'll show that old tub of a ship a clean pair of heels today. The day that Hood can't beat Renown on a good run is the day I'll resign my commission. There's tricks to running these engines that never appear in any book lad. For example…'

Pulver never got to hear what tricks the old engineer had in mind, because at that moment a crescendo of noises began to ring through their ears. The engine telegraph rang insistently and the telephone emergency call light began flashing. Seconds later those noises were overwhelmed by a sound that haunted the midshipman's memory for the rest of his life. The sound of metal screaming as it was torn beyond its strength.

The Renown had arrived.


Twelve inches of armour plate saved Pulver and Mr Roberts that day. It didn't save the three men who had the flesh flensed from them by high pressure steam. Nor did it save the two men crushed to death or the man flung to his death from a gantry.

H.M.S Renown, thirty-two thousand tons of steel, iron and brass moving at twelve knots hit Hood square on her stern. Pulver's extra knot had allowed her to hit Hood not on the starboard quarterdeck as history intended, but much further aft.

The Renown had been designed from the outset for ramming and that day it showed just how effective the tactic could be. The outer starboard propeller, all fifteen feet of it plus its supporting structure was ripped from the Hood, its mate the Starboard inner fared a little better but did far more damage to the Hood and Renown.

As Renown careered off the Hoods stern the inner propeller weakened from the impact lost two of its three blades. The first sliced through the Renown's forward torpedo blister, adding to her damage. The second blade, its base fractured flew through the water and five and a half tons of manganese bronze ripped into the Hoods rudder and embedded itself in its wooden core. The reduction gear of both shafts collapsed as they struggled and failed to balance forces that their designers had never envisaged.

Both drive shafts died that day, freed from the duty of driving the ship and still powered by the turbines they had a brief moment of mad liberty before burning out every bearing. Plates buckled, strakes and ribs shattered or twisted and the sea, suddenly triumphant, found a hundred new entry points and sent in advance parties to scout out its new domain.

Pulver did not sleep for the next two days, nor did any of the Hood's crew. Sleep was a luxury that their ship denied them. Damage had to be cleared, pumps rigged, great baulks of timber must take the place of ripped steel. Those two days taught him many things, the first was just how rich the English language was in swear words, the second was the knowledge that the Hood's crew were men who loved their ship and were determined not to lose her.

Tasks which should have taken days were completed in hours. Pulver thought that the men moved like dancers, never once stumbling, never for a moment getting in each other's way. Though as an untrained boy he was reduced to holding tools and fetching mugs of tea he never again felt unwanted and the oil stained grins he got from the men were truly humbling.

Finally as Hood and Renown were taken under tow and began to make their slow way back to port he was allowed to sleep.

As his head hit the pillow he realised there would be a court martial and that he may be called as a witness. He knew though with absolute certainty that his ship was doing exactly twelve knots.

# THE MARCH

It was the clock that triggered the whole thing.

It wasn't much of a clock, the varnish on the plain oak case had retreated to a few hard to reach areas and the steel mechanism showed definite signs of rust. At one stage it had happily marked the hours with a cheerful musical sound, but recently it too had succumbed to depression and had become mute apart from a wheezy creak at odd and unpredictable intervals.

To Geordie McIntyre the clock was more than a slightly unreliable time piece. It was a last link with happier times.

It was his wedding day clock.

'Why man you'll have little time to yourself after Saturday, so here's a little gift from us all to mark the day when your life ends'.

The scene from fifteen years ago was still fresh in his mind.

Old Billy McAlister grinning as he said the words and then a night lit only with blurry flashbacks as the lads took him to every pub they could think of.

For fifteen years the clock had celebrated Geordies life, births, deaths, anniversaries all had been marked and measured by the clock on the mantle -piece.

It was their last luxury.

His wife's wedding ring, worn so proudly had fed their family for a week. Geordies medals won at such a great cost had beaten off the rent man for a whole fortnight.

And now the clock had gone.

He knew without a shadow of doubt what had happened while he was out on another fruitless search for work. He angrily flung his cap and scarf onto the bare wooden chair.

'When?' He asked.

His wife wrung her hands with shame, the humiliation plain on her lined face.

'This morning, just after you'd left. I thought it was your mother, she said she'd pop round.' She began crying, the tears rolling down her face.

It was what every family in his street feared.

The Means Test.

'He just burst in', She continued, 'Not so much as a by your leave and began to open drawers and look in cupboards. I told him I'd sold my wedding ring already and your medals had gone. He didn't listen he just looked at the clock and said it was worth three pounds and made a note in his book and walked out.'

She began to sob now, great wracking sobs that seemed to shake her whole body.

'Oh Geordie I'm so sorry I thought it was your mother or I'd never have opened the door.'

'Three pounds?' Geordie thought, 'When it was new fifteen year ago it might just have been worth that...just, but now they'd be lucky to pledge it for ten shillings at Solomon's.'

His wife continued to sob and stammer out her apologies.

The undeserved shame in her voice made Geordie reach out and hold her.

'We'll be fine bonny lass. It just means we tighten our belts for a week or two that's all, no need to worry.'

He continued to murmur soothing words in her ear as he fought and failed to put out the fires of anger and fear that burnt hot and bright within him. There would be no dole for his family this week; the unemployment bureau would assume that this week he would have three pounds in his pocket. Three pounds that would never, indeed could never, exist.

Geordie McIntyre his wife and four children knew hardship, knew how to deal with it, how to subsist on potatoes and bread, how to pay one creditor one week and stay still as frightened rabbits when the others came knocking.

This they knew.

This was their life.

But now they faced actual deprivation, and that was a game in which the rules were totally different.

Altogether it was the most wretched half hour Ellen Wilkinson had experienced in a long time. The man stood there, cap in hand twisting it without even being aware that he was doing so, stammering out a tale that was both familiar and new at the same time. Two small girls stood behind him holding hands with an older boy who looked angry and ashamed without seeming to realise exactly why he was feeling that way.

A clock!

A bloody clock!

A family would be turned out of their home over a petty official's opinion of how much an old clock was worth. Of course she would help, of course the decision would be appealed and probably overturned, but that would take time. And it was all so unnecessary, the man standing before him was a skilled craftsman, easily capable of work if there was any to be had. Give the man half a chance, give him a second glance and he would grasp it with both hands and become a productive member of society.

And who knows what would happen then? Maybe those half-starved children could make something of themselves; at very least they might lose that half apathetic, half-starved look.

All over a bloody clock!

The family left with her assurances that she would act first thing tomorrow and two silver sixpences in each girl's right hand. It was the best she could do, and that fact angered her even more. She leaned back in her chair and lit a cigarette, sucking the smoke deep within her lungs with practiced ease and began to think.

Seven cigarettes later, and a read of yesterday's newspaper she had the beginnings of an idea. Reaching out for the telephone she began to dial.

It was the first of many calls she made that night.


'Of course I got it over turned, damn Jack in office couldn't back down quick enough once I turned up. That's the problem with this country today, too many people using other people's misery to feel important. You mark my words they'll come a day when the people...'

David Riley, the mayor of Jarrow held up a half humorous warning hand, stopping Wilkinson before she could launch into a political diatribe which he knew from experience could last for several minutes.

'Steady girl, steady, elections not yet and you're not on the hustings right now, we're all friends here.'

He paused and looked around the room. Businessmen, local politicians, and even a couple of clergymen, oddly enough sitting side by side. He grinned at Wilkinson, she would make a good MP for Jarrow when the time came.

'Alright so that red headed temper of yours put the fear of God into some poor bugger. It won't be the first time someone's gone home to change his undies after meeting you, and I doubt if it will be the last.'

A chuckle ran round the room. Everyone knew that Wilkinson was a passionate woman who was absolutely committed to her causes and had absolutely no qualms about trampling others to advance them. Wilkinson smiled a little at the interruption. The tall bull-necked man had come to know her well over the past few months.

'But this time it's different David, really it is. Look we can go around solving people's problems all day, all night for that matter, but it doesn't fix the main problem.'

'No work.' The voice came from the far corner of the room.

'Exactly, no work; but there is work out there.'

Riley shook his head.

'Aye lass there is, but none for Jarrow, do you not think we've tried? Letters, telegrams even petitions we've done them all. More than once sometimes.'

Wilkinson could see the frustration on his face and though bubbling with anticipation she let him continue. Scorn, born of long months of fruitless efforts had entered his voice.

'And what do we get?' *The matter is under consideration*, or *The minister regrets*. Jarrow will die; the people will die, or move, and there is nothing we can do about it.'

Wilkinson looked directly at him her voice now so soft as to be almost inaudible.

'I didn't come all this way to become MP to a dying town. There is a way to help this town and me and Geordie Macintyre are going to do it.'

She flung a day's old newspaper onto the table.

'There!'

Her voice had a touch of triumph in it now, as if she had won a major victory.

Riley looked at the article circled in black ink and the photographs showing two roughly patched warships leaving Gibraltar. Several other warships hovered around the battlecruisers like over anxious seagulls. The mayor raised a quizzical eyebrow.

'You're not thinking of us putting in a bid for the refit are you? For God's sake woman the shipyards closed down, the bloody receivers have sold every damn lathe, and they won't stop until everything has gone. We don't have a chance.'

A tall man with a clerical collar stood up and spoke with the easy assurance of someone who had enjoyed an exclusive and expensive education.

'I think that if Miss Wilkinson has an idea then we should at least listen to it before dismissing out of hand...if only out of politeness, after all as the mayor has said we are all friends here. Any plan for the relief of my parishioners has my interest.' He paused and took a visible deep breath before continuing. 'And very possibly my support.'

Wilkinson should hate James Gordon, the Bishop of Jarrow, because he represented everything that she had spent a lifetime trying to overcome, but she knew that he was a very effective advocate for the town's people. Quite simply his upbringing had given him an unshakable belief that he would be obeyed. And very often this soft, but unspoken attitude worked very well. She smiled therefore, recognising a potential ally in what she knew would be a series of hard-fought battles.

'Thank you Bishop. Yes David I think we should ask for the Shipyard to reopen and one of the ships to be refitted here. I think we should organise a march to London to publicise our cause.'

'Been tried lass, times without number and failed.' Riley's voice was gruff. 'Those bastards...'.he stuttered, mumbled an apology to the clergymen and began again. 'Those gentlemen in London don't give a tinkers curse how many times we march through Hyde Park or how many petitions we send.'

Wilkinson nodded.

'I agree, that's why when we march we don't take a petition. We take something far more powerful.'

Riley looked puzzled.

'What's more powerful than a petition?'

Wilkinson lit another cigarette and blew the smoke up to the ceiling, smiling broadly.

'Why gifts of course!'

Riley looked through the clouds of cigarette smoke at the grinning woman. *Gifts? Had the woman gone mad?*

Wilkinson continued to grin.

'Gifts David, gifts. One in particular. One very special gift, a gift so valuable that owning it almost destroyed a family.'

'Geordie McIntyre's clock?'

'Exactly. We don't make this march about Jarrow, we make it about Geordie.'

She stubbed out her cigarette in the overflowing ashtray.

'Gentleman, David was right, marches have failed before.' She listed other marches on her fingers ticking them off as she did so. 'The general strike in 1926...a failure. The 1927 Welsh hunger march...failure. The 1932 march... a failure with violence and riots. I could go on, you know I could go on. Every march not only failed in their objectives, but they actually harmed the very causes they wished to promote. And why? Because they were too big. Hundreds, thousands of men marching, begging for help. And they failed because some of those marches began and ended with violence.'

Riley opened his mouth to protest and Wilkinson knew that he was about to spring to the marchers' defence, but a warning cough from Bishop Gordon killed the protest before it could be born. She pretended not to see the interplay and continued.

'People, good people mostly, look at those marches and tell themselves that the problem is too big, too complex. And those good people think sad thoughts and move on with their lives. Or they read in the Daily Mail that the march is just another Bolshevik stunt and turn away. Either way the march fails. We cannot let that happen again. So we condense the problem, we make it not about a town or an industry, but about one man, one family. We use human nature, give the people a problem they can grasp, one they can feel. Let them identify with one man. We send Geordie down to London with his clock. Publicity is the key here. Geordie walks the length of the country and we tell his tale for him. Just us, the people of Jarrow, not the Labour Party, nor any other organisation. No interference, no compromises. Just us.'

A small thin man in a rumpled suit spoke. Wilkinson recognised him a local businessman; like many of his kind in Jarrow he hovered at the very edge of bankruptcy.

'Money', he said, 'It will still take money, even one man will need support. Where will that come from?' He seemed to shrink within his rumpled suit and gave her a bitter smile. 'There's not much money in Jarrow Miss Wilkinson.'

'And organisation', added Riley, 'If you are not going to involve anyone but us where is that going to come from? We can't use council funds that's for sure.'

'All that way?' Argued another voice, 'David's right, this isn't a day trip to the seaside here it would need planning, careful planning.'

Wilkinson's eyes were shining now, she had them arguing not over the idea, but over its practicality. She looked at the clergyman who sat next to the Protestant Bishop. The man was handsome she thought, almost a caricature of a kindly Catholic priest, but she knew that he was just as passionate a creature as she was, and far better than that, he had a genius for raising money. Schools, church buildings, charities all existed now in Jarrow because he had raised the money and shown the way. It was said, and only half in jest that the very curb stones bled shillings as Father Makin walked by. Significantly despite the rivalry between the denominations he had sat next to Bishop Gordon throughout the meeting. She hoped that was a good sign, as relations between Catholics and Protestants in Jarrow had never been good. She desperately needed his skills, so she was very careful with her words.

'I was hoping that the organisations that the churches have built up over the years could...'

She got no further.

Father Makin stood up and placed impressively large hands on the table which creaked alarmingly under the strain. With just a confirming glance at the bishop he spoke directly to Wilkinson with a half-smile on his lips which did not quite reach his eyes.

'So this is why you drag a half-retired priest across the country. Am I to have no peace? And how Miss Wilkinson are my parishioners, many of whom live from week to week, if not day to day supposed to afford the extra burden of sending a man and presumably some supporters three hundred miles south?'

It was a question that Wilkinson had no answer for. She had pinned her hopes on Makin's near legendary reputation.

'You raised money for your schools, Father, and the halls and the children's clubs and...'

Makin lifted his great paws from the table which almost sighed with relief.

'In better days Miss Wilkinson, in better days. You really have no idea how to raise the money locally?'

Wilkinson could only shake her head mutely. She had only half formed ideas, and she knew they could not compete with the expertise before her.

The priest nodded gravely.

'Well I do, and if this idea of yours is to succeed it seems as if I must drag myself into the fray once more, but my involvement does have a slight problem.'

There was a humorous cough from Bishop Gordon.

'Actually it's not so much a problem as an opportunity, a weapon perhaps that Father Makin has rather reluctantly dropped into my hand. Father Makin is well thought of by his superiors, he has a fund of good will to drawn on. I on the other hand, have no such fund. Indeed quite the opposite, many in the church hierarchy consider me to have dangerous radical tendencies.'

A wry smile was directed at Wilkinson as he continued. 'Despite my impeccable background. Now without going too deeply into Church politics I may be able to convince my superiors that allowing our rivals to gain ascendency in this matter would not be in our best long-term interests.'

He continued to look directly at Wilkinson, the smile long gone from his face.

'If this scheme is to be only the people of Jarrow with no outside agencies involved, then frankly I cannot see how the church can stand to one side.' He shook his head sadly, his voice now flat and stripped of emotion. 'Though I believe I can foresee a rather interesting future for me.'

Wilkinson realised that the bishop had just surrendered his chance of advancement in his church and done so without histrionics or drama, but calmly, almost casually as if his decision had no consequences worth mentioning. It was one of the bravest things she had ever seen, and it took a deliberate effort of will from her not to rush across the room and hug the man. Her plan had more than a chance now. With both churches backing her it would be very hard for any other group to resist joining in.

It was Riley who gave her the opportunity to reveal the rest of her plan.

'All very well lass sending down one man, but if Parliament can ignore a thousand men it will be easier still to ignore one man no matter how many clocks he takes with him.'

Wilkinson nodded, this was the very heart of her plan.

'Yes David. You are right, if we send Geordie to Parliament it will be a waste of good boot leather. But that's why Geordie isn't going to Parliament. He's going to see the King.'

She looked around the table suppressing a giggle which had been born from seeing so many shocked faces. If her idea worked then Geordie McIntyre had a long journey before him.

But before he could take a single step there was one more person to see.


The tea-leaves and the teapot were obviously old friends and unless Wilkinson missed her guess this was at least the third time that they had met. Still the gesture was a friendly one and though the tea was weak the conversation was lively. She knew that Geordie was a proud man and unemployment had hurt that pride. What she was asking him to do was exhibit his failure to provide for his family before the whole world. And that was a hard thing to ask of any man.

So she needed an ally, an ally that Geordie would not be able to resist, but now at the last moment she wondered if she had chosen wisely.

Mabel McIntyre was obviously a house-proud woman Wilkinson thought she would be hard pressed to find a single speck of dust in the house, and her door step and windows sparkled. Which made what she was about to ask all the harder, she should have realised that Mabel's pride would be the equal of her mates. Or maybe more than the equal, for she knew many men would have collapsed into apathy without their wives' stubborn pride.

She took a deep breath, prayed to every god she had ever heard off and began.

An hour later she had opened a seam of anger in Mabel which had surprised them both. Mabel had raged against the fates, emotions that had long been held hidden from her family spewed out in a hot torrent of anger and tears. There was now no doubt in Wilkinson's mind that whatever reservations Geordie may have would be swept away by a torrent of Mabel's newly released anger.

She had her man, and now there would be no stopping her.

The campaign for Jarrow had begun.


He was marching up to Arras with rifle and pack. Harry and Jack in front of him were laughing and joking about the red tabbed officer who had just ridden past them on a beautiful bay stallion.

'He's not a bad chap', Harry was saying.

'He's a bloody toff who looks like his horse's arse.'

Jack's reply drifted down the ranks causing little ripples of laughter to break out from the sweating men.

Geordie wasn't laughing there was something very urgent he needed to say to them, but he couldn't open his mouth. He tried and he tried, but all his efforts were unavailing, and what was upsetting was neither Harry nor Jack seemed to notice.

Then the scene shifted. It was night, a thin miserable rain was falling and Harry was missing, but Jack was in plain sight, two hundred yards away hung up on wire close to the German trenches.

And what was worse… alive.

They had no officers left, just a sergeant with a hole in his leg. Geordie knew what he had to do, but he was frightened, terrified in fact and strangely, oddly he knew that all the effort, all the danger would be wasted. He knew Jack would die tonight, so why was he doing this?

The crawl through mud took hours and he froze at every slight noise. The barbwire had wrapped around Jack in a very unfriendly embrace. He wasn't wasting words tonight though, again he had the feeling that he knew how the conversation would run.

'Aalreet Jack I've come te fetch yee back.'

The whispered reply was equally short.

'Divvent be bloody sackless yee idiot leave me be.'

There wasn't time for conversation.

'Shut up an dee as yer telt. Noo come wi me.'

He began to snip the wire, but as he did so the small bells attached to the wires were disturbed and began to jangle, adding their sharp metallic sounds to the muttering of the guns. A flare gun popped and the ground lit up like day, machine guns began to probe their fingers across the landscape. There was no time to waste now.

'On me back noo marra.'

There was a soft groan as he lifted Jack up now and he began to stumble through the mud, praying that he would not stumble, praying even harder that the German aim would be poor this night. Jack had been his friend since childhood so why was there a sense of failure hanging over him, why did he feel this was a waste of time? Bullets splashed into the mud around them, but he still put on foot in front of the other.

There was a soft chuckle from the body above him.

'Like a horse's arse, tha wez funny.'

Then there was silence broken only by Geordie's laboured lungs desperately sucking in the wet night air. The half broken, half held

24

British trenches had never looked so welcoming. But it was too late for Jack; a German bullet had severed the great artery in his left leg and his last words had been to recall a joke. Geordie had failed to rescue his friend...again.

He woke up, the scream ready to leap from his throat. Instinctively he reached out for Mabel, she would comfort him. She alone had the right words. But Mabel wasn't there and he realised that she would be missing from his bed for many a week to come.

He whimpered a little until the images faded. His nightmares had faded after he had married Mabel, or at least had come less frequently. It was the march that had triggered the memory, he was certain of that. And the excitement of the day of course.

A mass with Father Makin and his taking of the sacrament, the wafer dry upon his lips.

The presentation of his clock. Jakob Solomon of all people handing over his clock and ripping up the pawn ticket with a great flourish and a smile which was only half forced. The crowd had cheered at that, though privately Geordie thought that the change of heart was all too temporary.

David Riley made a speech thanking the people of Jarrow for their support, telling them that every penny would help speed Geordie on his way, and hopefully bring the day when Jarrow would live again. Then Geordie was blessed by Bishop Gordon as a special emissary of Jarrow. Father Makin had fumed over this and impressed on Geordie that the Church considered the blessing to have no value and it was his personal view that accepting the blessing was perilously close to being a sin. However Makin's own bishop over ruled him and the priest confined himself to scowling while the blessing was made. It was only fair thought Geordie; the Protestants had entered the race to raise money with passion and they deserved to take part. He would never tell Father Makin that though; he had too much respect for the priest's temper to ever risk his soul over such an errant thought.

And so he had taken first steps on the road that led out of Jarrow, putting one foot in front of the other just as he had that day on the road to Arras.

Left, right, swing the arms.

Left, right, swing the arms.

The old rhythms coming back naturally, and strangely enough bringing him a measure of comfort.

But not enough. Not nearly enough. The old nightmare, the old fears had returned. And Mabel not there to help.

He stared at the lime washed bedroom ceiling of the first cheap boarding house room of his journey. No Mabel meant that his demons must be quelled without her. No matter how many times he took that journey through the mud Jack was still dead. There was no magic formula that would resurrect him. He'd tried once back in 1916 and failed, and even in failure they'd given him a medal for the attempt. He blinked several times as a thought sprang into instant life.

Now he understood.

Now he understood how to kill his own demons, how to utterly extinguish them.

He saw that he was on another rescue mission, one that had more than one life to save. He was brave last time when he only faced bullets; he could be brave this time when the stakes were higher. He smiled as sleep began to reclaim him. His march would continue. For along as it took

Jack would approve. Of that he was sure.


There was only the march. He was long weeks now from that first night and that last nightmare. Geordie's world had narrowed. There was only the march.

Left, right, swing the arms.

It stretched out before him and behind him.

Left, right, swing the arms.

Weeks now.

Left, right, swing the arms.

The straps of his pack had worn grooves in his shoulders.

Left, right, swing the arms.

His boots rang on the tarmac transmitting shocks to legs which had long since forgotten how to receive them.

Left, right, swing the arms.

The rain ran down his face, each greasy drop dragging the sweat from a face which framed unseeing eyes.

Left, right, swing the arms.

Mile merging seamlessly into mile. Un-noticed, unheralded.

Left, right, swing the arms.

There was only the march.

He had conversations in his head. Mabel and the bairns of course. Father Makin; stern and uncompromising. And the dead.

The dead appeared often, perhaps because they were phantoms that he could mould, perhaps because they were less threatening than the living. He tried to explain to them, convince them, cajole them into acceptance of what he was doing. The dead walked with him joking or serious, happy or sad as he remembered them. They walked with him pace for pace, never tiring, tempering the isolation he felt.

As he walked south even the towns failed to quench the solitude. He remembered one town now days behind him that had welcomed him with banners and bands. They gave him lunch with speeches. The speeches meant nothing to him, but the lunch had surprised him and shocked his hosts. He recalled staring at the sandwich and sniffing at it suspiciously, then gingerly opening it as if a wild thing lay within. He had grunted with satisfaction as the contents were revealed. It was exactly as he expected, and he knew at once just what he had to do, as man, but more importantly as a husband and a father. He opened his pack and removed one of the pre-addressed envelopes that Ellen Wilkinson had given him weeks before. His hosts looked on with astonishment as he removed the slice of ham from the sandwich and carefully placed it in the envelope.

'For the bairns.' He had explained. 'They haven't tasted meat since Christmas, I'll post this as a treat.'

He ignored the looks of shock. What else was a man supposed to do?

Jack, dead these past twenty years had stood by him laughing.

'Man that shook them, sandwiches by post.'

'Now they know.' Replied Geordie grimly as he left the town.

There was only the march.

Left, right, swing the arms.

It stretched out before him and behind him.

Left, right, swing the arms.

Towns passed him, villages strolled by.

Left, right, swing the arms.

Reporters jostled him, probed and questioned him, always seeking that final answer, always seeking to trap him and expose him. It was then that Mabel leapt from his imagination and stood by his side. It was her words and her spirit that scattered his tormentors and answered his supporters.

Left, right, swing the arms.

Always there were the tawdry boarding houses, the same damp sheets, the same whitewashed ceilings where only the cracks varied. Sometimes there was a welcoming committee. Other times he passed through ignored or unwelcome, but the rhythm of the road always beat inside his head.

Left, right, swing the arms.

Outside the world changed. A Prime Minister resigned. Two battered warships pulled up to receiving, welcoming wharfs. A minor point in an agreement resulted in Germany walking away from a naval treaty. Spain lurched to the right and then the left, rebellions and strikes stalked her land. Italy advanced her preparations to invade Abyssinia. But for Geordie the world consisted only of the sound of his boots and the voices in his head.

It was the signpost that stopped him more than the more crowded roads and more populous streets. It took a few moments for the significance of the sign to penetrate his fatigued mind. But eventually the black painted letters formed a single word.

London.


Ellen Wilkinson put down the phone, relief and triumph fighting for supremacy on her face.

'London, just on thirty miles from Westminster.'

Father Makin grumbled 'Six weeks without confession or Mass, that can't be good for him.'

A gently mocking smile fell from Bishop Gordon's face.

'Think of it as a pilgrimage, surely that will be equally good for his soul?'

David Riley, exercising a now finely-honed sense of danger spoke very quickly before Father Makin and the Bishop began to once more trade theological insults.

'That's excellent news Ellen. So now Geordie asks for an audience?'

Wilkinson nodded, grateful for the mayor's diplomacy.

'The request has already gone out, very, very formal and sent out via the right channels. We'll let Geordie rest for a few days, and then we start the next stage.'

She grinned, relishing the thoughts that ran through her head.

'But it's only the beginning. With the election in a few months this is the ideal time to apply pressure. We keep on applying pressure, we never, ever let up, we can't, we're in too deep now. We can win, I know we can win. Geordie's done well, the publicity has been better than I expected, when the papers picked up the story we began to win. But our best victory I didn't anticipate.'

Riley chuckled.

'What sort of people are we?'

Geordie's mailing back a single slice of ham had so upset the mayor of Leicester that he wrote to The Times and asked angry rhetorical questions. As political storms went it wasn't a hurricane - more a minor downpour - but Wilkinson seized upon it and ensured that the government was thoroughly dampened. Riley continued chuckling.

'Put a few noses out of joint that letter, the Daily Mail accused him of being a Bolshevik stooge of course, but the debate was interesting. It seems that not every reader of the Times is a rapacious Tory.'

Bishop Gordon spoke, a sad tone in his voice.

'And we need more of that sort of thing, I don't know where you will find them, but find them you must, and Ellen you must find them without me.'

The sadness in his voice was now mirrored in his face.

'It seems that my last letter to the Times was a move to far. I've been invited to lunch at Lambeth Palace. I rather suspect that a discreet telling off is in my future, followed by an appointment to where I can do no harm.'

Wilkinson felt the tears form in her eyes.

'Oh James!' She cried and rushed to give him a long-delayed hug.

He seemed a little embarrassed at this display of affection.

'We all knew this would happen - we knew from the first moment, so this should come as no surprise. I'll leave now if I may, I have some packing still to do.'

As he shook hands with everyone Wilkinson realised that the first blow against her had been struck. She knew that there would be others, and that battle had been joined. She prayed that she would be granted victory. She prayed that Geordie would not fail her. But for her the battle would go on. For her party. For the people of Jarrow.

And nothing would stand before her.

# HOME

Ministers it was said were the holders of power, but the men who had gathered around the table knew that ministers were merely holders of office and temporary ones at that. It was they who wielded power. Power to influence, and the ultimate power...that of decision.

They were all of a type these men. All of them had attended a good preparatory school and then spent a few years at a public school. And after that a degree in something safe; classics was always popular, preferably at Winchester, but Oxford or Cambridge were almost as good. Then the civil service exams and a slow steady rise through the ranks. An induction into the right clubs followed and if all went well a companionship into the order of Saint Michael and Saint George at forty and upon retirement a knighthood in the same order. And finally a life at a genteel spa town Cheltenham or Bath perhaps or for the truly rebellious a small villa on the Bournemouth seafront. Theirs was a life of calm, cerebral discussion, of careful weighing of every aspect of a situation.

Situations like today's where there were competing claims for scarce resources needed such an approach. It was one particular man's task to begin to solve a problem which had many aspects and was only on the surface a military problem. He liked to think of himself of the first amongst equals or in his darker moments as the most unfortunate of his group. For his sins, which he sardonically thought were obviously heavy and of long standing, he represented the Prime Minister at these meetings.

He had climbed to the very top of the greasy pole. There were times though when he wondered if the view was worth the aggravation. Perhaps it was time to seriously consider whether a seaside vista might be a more pleasant experience than the view of Ten Downing Street's garden shed?

He grimaced at the weak tea, noting the teacup had a tiny chip and munched on a damp arrowroot biscuit. Time was when the tea would be served in the very best China and the biscuits would be chocolate bourbons or at the very least custard crèmes. But times were hard these days and everyone was expected to make sacrifices, even senior civil servants. He sighed, put the tea cup down without regret and brought the meeting to order.

'Well let us begin. The recent mishap in the Mediterranean fleet has caused certain assumptions to be reassessed and certain realities to be faced. The Navy now faces a future where two of its capital ships are no longer available, and if initial reports are to be given credence both will require extensive repairs. While it is true that one of those ships was scheduled for some form of refit this was not due until the next financial year.'

He smiled acknowledging that the technical details were beyond him and then repeated the last few words slowly and clearly, so their impact was clear. 'Was...not...due...in...this...financial...year. And that Gentlemen brings us neatly to the first of the problems which face us.

'Foreign policy implications, industrial capacity, tactical and strategic problems apart; indeed all other considerations placed to one side. Just how will we fund the upgrades which the Navy has suggested, indeed more than suggested are required for these ships? In other words just what is the Navy willing to forgo in order to gain its objectives?'

He smiled benignly around the room waiting for one of his colleagues to speak first, but they knew the game as well as he did. The first to speak revealed too much and was preyed upon by those who had left their guns masked. As the smile faded from his face he realised that once more he would be forced to be chooser of the slain. He fixed the War Ministry with a blank look.

'James this is your area I believe, perhaps you could start here.'

As the man reluctantly began to speak he began to wonder if this conversation would take a different form if they knew what he had been told this morning. Ramsey McDonald the long ailing, increasingly incoherent Prime Minister had informed him that today he had decided to resign. In a few months there would be a General election. In a few months all might change. Politically of course.

In his world there was no change. No change at all.


He wasn't a fighting admiral. He'd never walk on a quarter deck, nor sleep in an admiral's cabin. The sea would always be a stranger to him and gunnery would forever be a mystery. But he'd fought more battles than any ten sea going admirals combined, and what was more he'd won most of them. Without him ships would sail infrequently, or not at all and crews would be reduced or disappear entirely. He was a political admiral and proud to be so.

Not for him the thunder of the guns or the sudden surge through the waves. His weapons were more subtle, though equally or perhaps more deadly than the gun or the torpedo. He flailed his enemies with soft words or deadly statistics. He had no allies in his battles, only those who for a time could be persuaded, though never trusted. He knew them all, these temporary partners; politicians, journalists, diplomats and of course the ultimate power brokers, the civil servants.

His web ranged far and wide and it was he who had asked for a temporary delay in signing a naval treaty with Germany. The navy had lost a combined hundred thousand tons of very important warships and therefore it seemed right that the German allowance be cut back to recognise that. Much as he had expected Berlin did not agree to the delay and talks were in abeyance while the treaty remained unsigned. His reluctant ally the Foreign Office had gulped nervously but had remained steadfast. It was as much as he could manage at this point - a victory, but a small one.

He was sure that his French counterparts would be pleased, even if he trusted them even less than any other potential ally. The treasury though had screamed like a nervous virgin; they had no intention of funding a building war with Germany and were not hesitant in saying so. Still he and his reluctant ally had no intention of seeing British influence diminished by a Germany that was showing disturbing signs of stretching its muscles once more even though the treasury had influence too, that could not be denied, so he must give his political allies ammunition with which to fight their battles.

He flipped open the first of the folders with sigh. Ships, men, bases, projects, designs and dreams appeared before him, reduced to typed summaries of a paragraph or less. All lay within his power, all trembled at the brink of extinction. He picked up an ornate fountain pen ,filled it with red ink and began to write.

And condemned a Battlecruiser to death.

The hum of the generator gave out a sad, subdued hum. It still did its duty, but reluctantly, almost as if it knew that soon it would be stilled for a long time to come.

The Hood had been emptied. Spanners and hammers, bullets and beef, shells and socks all had been noted and stored away in warehouses. She rode higher in the water now, bereft of men and stores, still a beautiful ship, but no longer a fighting one.

Pulver and the Chief engineer took one last walk through their kingdom. Her scars were still evident; plates and ugly ironwork had been hastily welded to stop further collapse. The normal cathedral like spaces were now filled with interlinked girders, functional no doubt, but so very ugly. Though she was tied up securely the Hood's engine rooms were filled with groans and squeaks as the repairs struggled with the loads placed upon them.

'She doesn't like it Mr Pulver, listen to her complain.'

The Engineer's voice was sympathetic, full of concern for the ship he loved.

Pulver understood. He felt the same way, the ship felt nervous somehow, as if it faced an uncertain future over which it had no control.

'But she'll be repaired sir, the Captain said as much.'

'Aye that he did, but the Captain has no more say in the matter than you or me.'

The dour Scottish face brightened, a rare smile cracking the lined face. 'But you'll be fine whatever happens Mr Pulver. It's engineering school for you, and possibly a fine career to come.'

Pulver blushed, he'd not seen the recommendations that the Engineer and the First Lieutenant had written, but his application to become an engineer had been approved almost by return of post which he knew was almost unheard of in the Navy. He was about to stammer out his thanks, but the Engineer turned on his heel and began the long journey to the upper deck.

Two hours later a hand turned a switch and the generator muttered and died.

The Hood began her long sleep.

# ELECTION

This year, this election was the one.

This one, Wilkinson thought was the one where she became an MP. This was the year jobs returned to Jarrow. There were speeches to be made, hands to shake, promises to give. All this and more to be done before the last vote could be counted. But most important of all was the campaign built around one man.

Geordie McIntyre.

.

The sound of Big Ben floated through the air. It gathered round and enveloped the man as he walked with a long practiced loping stride that gave the maximum of distance with the minimum of effort. He crossed the last few yards towards the ornate iron gates and came to a complete halt, stiffened and with absolute military precision saluted the ancient building. Then as he had done so many times before he opened a weathered canvas bag and with exaggerated care removed a battered clock and held it aloft.

Fifteen minutes later as the quarter hour struck the clock was returned to its home and to the obvious disappointment of the many tourists that surrounded him he retraced his steps and retreated, a small knot of people following him like a comets tail.

Two men, a king and his Prime Minister stood discreetly behind the curtains of Buckingham Palace and watched Geordie McIntyre.

'He'll be back, give him three quarters of an hour and the entire process repeats.'

King George's voice had changed over the years, becoming less powerful as age and disease took its toll. Today, as well as the fragility of age the voice had tones of gloom and anger.

'Damn it Baldwin the man's a blasted nuisance, he's besieging me in my own home. If I accede to his request for a visit and accept that damned clock, I can't give him what he wants, and in any case if I do open my door to him I'll have every beggar in the country wanting to visit and that simply won't do. The man has vowed to follow me wherever I go, it's simply intolerable, and people are beginning to ask questions, embarrassing questions. Just have the man arrested, that will be an end of him and I can return to some semblance of normality.'

He brightened a little as a thought struck him.

'He must be breaking some law, find one and use it.'

A wheezy laugh accompanied the thought, but the Prime Ministers reply was melancholy.

'I'm afraid that won't do, Your Majesty. Entertaining as the thought is the plain fact of the matter is that this man now has a following, and even if he hadn't, the advice I've been given is that arresting the man is simply impossible. Legally he's entirely within his rights to do exactly as he pleases.'

Baldwin knew the answer would not please the old king and the explosion was everything he expected.

'Well it doesn't please me. Do something before this whole situation blows up in my face. I'm being dragged into the political arena and made a laughing stock. Buy the man off, arrest him, whatever you think best, but do it soon.'

Baldwin nodded agreement, the king was undoubtedly right, and action needed to be taken, but not for the reasons the outraged king gave. Far more important events were being influenced by the man from Jarrow.

Voters were strange creatures when all was said and done, prone to strange fancies, and Geordie had taken their fancy and worse excited their sympathy. A subtle and skilled publicity campaign had placed him in the public eye, the BBC much to Baldwin's fury had interviewed him and Pathé News had done a whole news reel on Jarrow. It only needed an extra push and the campaign could become a real problem.

And that must not happen.

Geordie McIntyre must be stopped.

Now.


The man himself was the message Wilkinson thought.

Ernest Bevan was a pillar of the Labour Party and hated communists with a passion. And she was a former communist and therefore his enemy, or at the very least someone to be treated with great suspicion. And yet the leader of Britain's greatest trade union had met her here to ask her a question which on the surface was deceptively simple. The hulking man with the broad West Country accent and bull neck had phrased it in his typically blunt manner.

'We've had enough of him, him and his bloody airs and graces and his bloody conscience. We don't stand a chance in the election with him as leader and that's a fact.'

The *him* in question was George Lansbury, the man who had led the Labour party for the past four years. His genuine and lifelong pacifism had always sat uneasily with certain factions within the party and now it looked as if those factions had combined under Clement Attlee to unseat him. Wilkinson was not at first glance a natural choice to join the coup; she was sympathetic to Lansbury's devotion to world peace and the man was a personal friend.

And that was the first problem.

Wilkinson was in the middle of a campaign to bring a warship to Jarrow and Attlee had seen not only her pragmatic ability to sacrifice her inclinations towards the greater good, but her skills in publicity and public speaking. Sending down his chief ally, a man from the right wing of the party to see her was a sign of just how important she had become. It was flattery no doubt, but his regard was based on the success of Geordies march. If she joined Attlee, then he could claim a broad support, not just from the right-wing unions which already backed him. And Bevan had promised much more.

And that was the second problem.

Overturning years of apathy and active opposition some unions, seeing just what Geordie had achieved had a last offered help and support. It was an offer, a risk and very possibly a threat.

The offer was welcome. Even Father Makin's legendary money raising powers were being stretched to their limits and union support meant that Jarrow which had given so generously could accept some relief.

Geordie though was the public face of Jarrow. Geordie was why they and many others supported him and took him into their hearts. He was the underdog, a David fighting a faceless uncaring Goliath. Having the overt backing of unions would destroy his credibility and a fickle public could soon turn from him, and his borrowed power would be lost.

And then there was the threat, unstated, but none the less very real, that Geordie, or at least the name and reputation that had been so carefully built up around him would be used regardless of whether she agreed or not.

So here she was sitting across the table from her political opposite debating her options, deciding if this man was an attack dog or an emissary bearing gifts. Deciding if she needed them as much as they needed her. Deciding if they really did need her. Deciding if she could betray her friend, and if she could salve her conscience. Deciding if she could use this opportunity to help Jarrow, and herself. She took a deep breath and looked at the unsmiling man before her.

'I'd want a portfolio.'

A tiny flicker crossed Bevan's face.

'Which one did you have in mind?'


Mabel McIntyre had been tempted. The devil had spoken to her in a silky-smooth voice.

Ellen Wilkinson had sat down in her best chair and read the letter that Mabel had given her. It was an impressive letter, delicately typed on headed notepaper. It was also an unsubtle bribe. It offered Geordie a job, a job far from Jarrow, well paid and secure.

'Your family will be safe', The Devil had whispered. 'Isn't this what Geordie is fighting for? Take it, take it now, and never look back.'

The voice pleaded with her, pride doing battle with her instinct to protect her family. Her hands had shaken as she poured tea into Wilkinson's cup. Her instincts were surrendering slowly but surely as the devil's justifications took hold. But her pride took renewed strength and with indomitable power thrust the devil from the room. With barely contained anger she rejected the letter, tearing it to shreds in front of an astonished Wilkinson. She had vowed that she would never allow Geordie to give in, that she would rather die than disappoint the people of Jarrow. But now the devil had extracted revenge for his expulsion.

Her son, her first born had reached an age where government relief would no longer be paid and on his fourteenth birthday must leave home. He was taking a route many a Jarrow boy had taken by walking into the arms of the Navy.

She held back her tears and contented herself with a long litany of cautions and warnings that continued right up the moment that the guards whistle cut her admonishments in two.

She had lost the second man in her life.

And the devil laughed.


The cadence was hypnotising as the great steel wheels drove over the rails. One, two, three, four, one, two, three, four.

Outside hot steam fought bravely against frigid air and then dispersed over the scattered houses and hamlets. No passengers slept in this speeding train, no anxious business men, harried mothers, or joyful holiday makers. This train was a sinew of a nation, a nerve that ran down the great spine of the country.

This was the Night Mail.

All other trains bowed before it. It alone had right of way. It alone bore the red livery of the Royal Mail.

Inside, legions of men shouted arcane incantations as they rapidly placed letters in thousands of slots. Order and sense were being fashioned out of chaos and confusion. Only the front carriage was empty, empty but for two men and a strange net like contraption which clung like a spider's web to the side of the carriage.

The two men were silent, old hands at this game. They were expectant, arms held loosely by their sides. Only their mouths moved silently in time with the cadence of the wheels.

One, two, three, four, one, two, three, four.

A muffled whoosh as they ran under a bridge.

One, two, three, four, one, two, three, four.

The cadence slowed a little as she climbed.

A second whoosh and...

Bang!

A heavy canvas and leather bag was catapulted into their arms; ripped from the awaiting post by the speed of the train. The two men dived on the bag like starving seagulls, opening the straps and bindings that protected the precious cargo that lay within. They too began to mutter words as they roughly sorted the mail. As they did so a muffled ringing came from one of the parcels causing one of the men to giggle a little.

'Another clock for old Baldwin there Charlie. How many do you think he's got now?'

His friend a dour older Cockney replied in his normal lugubrious manner.

'Must be a few thousand now Fred. A few thousand easy. All I knows is that mail to Downing Street and the King has gone up considerable since they started that campaign.'

He quoted directly from the posters that had sprung up overnight.

'Send them clocks.'

'How's that supposed to change things. It's only going to get old Baldwin's back up.'

Charlie disagreed.

'No mate it's just asking him to change his mind a little that's all. He can ignore letters and petitions, but a few ton of clocks delivered to his door ain't so easy to ignore.'

He grinned exposing tobacco stained teeth.

'And it gets in the papers. Anyway it's work for us, Fred and overtime as well. Your missus will be pleased with that, keep you out of the pub at least.'

Fred grunted dismissively as he hoisted the sack of mail onto his shoulder.

'No chance of that Charlie no chance at all.'

And Geordie McIntyre's campaign rolled on.

One, two, three, four, one, two, three, four.


The king had retreated to his Sandringham estate, doggedly pursued by Geordie, his clock and a growing crowd of supporters and reporters.

Lansbury had resigned, faced with overwhelming fire power from every flank. He had surrendered with a grace and dignity that had left Wilkinson shamed. She tried to bury the memory with work and threw herself into the fray with all her energy. And today as she looked at the first run of new posters she nodded with approval. They were bold without being garish, tasteful without being bland.

The first showed Geordie's clock with *It's time to vote Labour* embossed over it in bright red letters. The second post showed a long line of tired looking men stretching off into the distance. *National isn't working* read the inscription. The third, which was her favourite showed a picture of an exhausted looking Geordie holding up his clock. *How many more?* the poster asked. She hoped it was a question many would ask themselves. Because every vote counted.

Every vote counted…if Jarrow was to be saved.


The view from the Prime Minister's office was bleak. Last night's early autumn gale had stripped not only the early red leaves from the trees, but also the more resolute green ones. This morning both varieties lay in confusion on the lawn.

Baldwin refused to accept the resemblance between his election campaign and the scene that the damp grass presented, but if he was honest he would admit he had been caught off balance. The problem was there was always a comedian; it did not matter where he spoke or for how long, there was always someone to ask if he knew the time. The joke was never that funny and had long since passed into the realm of desperately unfunny. Of course he always replied that it was time to vote for the local Conservative candidate, but the reply never seemed to garner the laughs that the question evoked.

Innumerable clocks had been delivered to his office. Large clocks, small clocks, pocket watches, even on one occasion a grandfather clock, though mercifully that had arrived without a mechanism. It was not the clocks themselves that mattered to him. It was the organisation and the opinions behind those clocks that worried him. One man did not traverse the length of the country without backing, and that one man had achieved in his journey what thousands of others failed to do. He had attracted the attention of the all-important middle ground. And that was where political wars were won.

Voters were beginning to question government policies now that they had a sharp and very visible example of them before their eyes. Well he had been caught by surprise, the clocks were a potent weapon that had exposed a weakness in his armour.

He blinked for a moment weighing options, deciding probabilities, but really there was no alternative. He would still play to his strengths. He would still tell the voters that he was the cautious helmsmen and the stars he would steer by would be the League of Nations and collective security, his experience and wisdom would become even more central to the campaign.

That said the Labour campaign was a threat and must be blunted.

Documents would be written, and messages sent. He hated policy changes in the middle of a campaign.

But he hated losing even more.


It wasn't the victory Ellen Wilkinson had hoped for, but it was still a victory, and more importantly it wasn't the result that their opponents wanted.

Geordie was on his way home. He had pursued the king with all the dogged tenacity that had won him medals twenty years before. At last a compromise had been reached; the Prince of Wales would accept the clock on behalf of his father and pass on the message from the people of Jarrow.

Wilkinson never doubted that this scheme came from the able mind of the Prime Minister, but also was more than half convinced that the young Prince relished the chance to score points against his father. The Prince had mentioned that he wished to visit Jarrow though this would be far into the future and in any case if the rumours were true he would be far too busy with more personal matters. But regardless of Baldwin's schemes, regardless of the Prince's war with his father, or who he chose to be his bed mate, Geordie was returning home wreathed with the laurels of victory. Jarrow was back on the political map and she was determined to ensure that it stayed there.

Because Baldwin had blinked.

It wasn't much of a blink, but again that wasn't the point, in war forcing your opponent to retreat was the first step in forcing him to retreat further.

*A possible small expansion of industrial capacity* was now the phrase being used by every government politician who had tried to claim responsibility for this miniscule change of heart. It was a start and her party was pushing hard to pin Baldwin down as to exactly what the phrase meant.

The Conservatives had hoped to remove Geordie as a weapon, believing that they had removed a potent sting from their adversary, but it was too late. Wilkinson and her staff had found new ways to use the broad-shouldered man from the back streets of Jarrow.

A new series of posters appeared.

*No clock and no work* was simple and to the point, and a picture of Geordies calloused hands was joined with the words *let these hands work* which was more emotive and also more effective.

Better yet the people of Jarrow still benefited from Geordie. The Labour party had pledged that every image of Geordie that they used would result in a payment being made for the relief of poverty in the town. Both sides won, both had succeeded in gaining what they needed.

But posters, even Geordie himself, could not break Baldwin's hold on power.

Much to Wilkinson's annoyance there were very few speeches where what she considered the true socialist message was delivered. Instead, in speech after speech Attlee and every Labour candidate had hammered home the message that Labour was ready for government and was the sensible choice. It was infuriating to realise that Attlee was right; men like Geordie, women like the house-proud Mabel, would vote for Labour regardless now. But there were not enough Geordies and Mabel's and never would be.

Where the election would be won would be in the soft middle ground, the undecided fearful men and women who were just surviving, just making ends meet. The men and women who read newspapers and looked at Europe with distaste and wanted no further part in it. Convincing them that small changes would be beneficial and no threat to them, that aiding men like Geordie was good for the country, was the very essence of the campaign.

Despite her distaste for Attlee she recognised that his pragmatism was the only way to win and the only way for her to rise.

But it was still frustrating.

Today was the day.

Election day.

Geordie and Mabel stood patiently in line at the local school. Despite waking early and walking the short distance to the school they still found the queue stretched out beyond the school gates. It was obvious that all of Jarrow was out to vote this morning. So they stood wrapped in their breath, stamping their feet against the winter cold.

Geordie nodded to a few of his friends. They were men. No other communication was required.

Mabel though had no idea of being reticent this day; she and the other women chattered over, around and through each other. Who had married, who had died, who was pregnant and who wasn't, who was doing well and who wasn't.

Geordie caught a fragment of conversation about his son, Jack who had joined the Navy. He heard the pride in his wife's voice as she told of how much the Navy thought of him. To hear her speak he would be an admiral before the week ended, but he too had read his son's letters and was secretly proud as well.

All morning the queue shuffled forward in the biting damp. For this was the day.

Election day.

And while the cold bit, and while they shivered, Europe writhed with new found energy. And while they held the ballot papers in their hands men in Germany were gathering to sign papers which would only two days hence announce to the world the birth of battleship 'F'.

It was an unassuming name for such a powerful ship, perhaps deliberately so. But one day battleship 'F' would be known by another name.

Bismarck.

# TEA AND SYMPATHY

The balloons and the streamers were liars. They told tales of victory and success. They hung gaily from the ceiling mocking her hopes.

Ellen Wilkinson held her head which throbbed to a rhythm all of its own. Despite the pain she grinned just a little, it had been quite a party. But it was not a party which celebrated total victory, for that had been denied them. Stanley Baldwin would form a government, a government with a paper-thin majority, but a government nether the less. The Liberal party, despite a further slide in popularity, would give sufficient support to the Conservatives so that they could survive.

But they would not govern in comfort.

Attlee had been very certain about that; a tiny majority was not a sure shield. His voice over the phone was as dry and emotionless as ever. He saw the election not as a defeat but a series of successes. Their rivals had been reduced and the Liberals had failed to benefit from their demise as they had hoped. And in the local elections more towns and cities had fallen to Labour, and where Wilkinson had felt disappointment and frustration Attlee had seen only opportunity. Baldwin, he had said would be given no respite and no comfort, he and his government would from the first day be denied any sense of security.

As the conversation ended with a soft click Wilkinson knew that she had many battles ahead of her. Because as of today she was not only a newly elected MP but was part of Attlee's shadow cabinet. The people of Jarrow had just elected someone who had vowed to fight for them and Attlee had now put her in the front rank and thrust a weapon into her hands.

And she fully intended to use it.


The winter of 1936 had been hard Baldwin thought. They'd buried a king and acquired another. Germany walked a little faster towards gaining full military strength. Spain elected a new left -wing government. Italy commenced her final campaign in the conquest of Abyssinia. All of these events had caused him sleepless nights and he was sure would cause even more as the year progressed, but he'd faced his first true domestic challenge and had won.

He was certain of that.

His government had achieved a strange sort of trembling stability. It had too many inexperienced members promoted before they were truly ready, that was certainly true. It had ministers and secretaries who owed their positions not to their ability, but because that was the price he had to pay for their parties' support. Managing this was occasionally difficult; it took time and effort but was an accepted part of managing a coalition government. What had been more difficult was managing his own party and fending off a confident opposition who took every chance to make his task more difficult.

The pattern was clear now.

Attack dogs, Ellen Wilkinson chief amongst them constantly savaged his policies opening up wounds which Attlee with mordant wit then proceeded to carve up with unconcealed glee.

He'd lost Samuel Hoare that way.

As Foreign Secretary he had proposed an agreement where the governments of both the United Kingdom and France recognised the greater part of Italy's gains in her war with Abyssinia. It was entirely the wrong idea.

The public, despite still having an almost pathological desire to avoid conflict reared up on its collective hind legs and roared its disapproval. In France, the government facing an even more virulent reaction actually fell and renewed itself under Leon Blum as a provisional administration. But it was here, here in Westminster that his problems lay.

As he had expected the opposition benches had taken the public anger, fashioned it into barbs and flung it with disturbing and painful accuracy into the ranks of his government. But not all of the ranks.

Some of his MPs had openly defied him over the issue, using it not only to protect themselves from the wrath of their electorates, but to force changes in government foreign policy.

And they had tasted victory.

One of their number, the dapper Antony Eden had taken Samuel Hoare's place. He intended to ensure that that he took more direct control of how his country acted in the world. Eden would find that he was foreign secretary in name only and would see his victory turn to ashes in his mouth. From now on foreign policy would be decided here in Ten Downing Street not at the Foreign Office. It was better he thought to make his enemy his servant and that was why he had allowed his rebels their victory.

He smiled as he realised that he managed to covert a potential split in his party into an act which had only strengthened his hold on the country. He was still the master politician he told himself.

He was so pleased with himself that he quite forgot that this afternoon one of the Labour back benchers had asked an apparently innocuous question about steel tariffs.

For Geordie's campaign had not ended with the election.


It was a four-ale pub in the back streets of Birmingham, sufficiently obscure Wilkinson hoped to cover any news of this meeting leaking out.

At least for now.

They had invited the leaders of Britain's steel industry to this backroom hoping that there would be, if not a meeting of minds then at least a recognition that there could be an opening that both could exploit. This, as far as she was concerned was consorting with the enemy but the big man beside her had given her no option and besides if they were ever to form a government people like this would be a part of it. So she sat in dingy room, Ernest Bevan beside her, sipping bottled lemonade through a straw, watching the men on the other side of the table sip at cheap whisky, while the roar of the Saturday night crowd crept into the room like a stealthy thief. By the look on their faces the whiskey was not to their taste or perhaps it was the offer they had just heard.

That they had been intrigued enough to come to the meeting in the first place was a good sign of course, but then again given the situation they faced what choice did they have? To be honest they weren't the rabid plutocrats Wilkinson had imagined; they were small men with a faint air of desperation about them. The past few years had been hard on them.

Cheap subsidised steel had begun to flow into the country at a time when demand for steel was plummeting. Small steel firms had failed or been swallowed up by larger firms who later regretted doing so. Nervous banks had been less then helpful, but despite that many had survived, albeit in a shaky fashion. Now they faced other threats, threats which could see an even steeper decline.

It was just the opening the Labour Party had been looking for, and Wilkinson and Bevan had been sent to try and show them a way to turn their problems to advantages. She smiled seeking to reassure them, hoping that her good humour would cut through the pub's atmosphere of stale beer and vomit.

'Gentleman this is a good offer and it's an opportunity.'

'No it isn't.'

The flat denial did not wipe the smile from her face, she was far too good a politician for that, but it did make her realise that these talks were going to be far harder than she had imagined. Obviously, the leaders of the British steel firms would take some convincing.

The big man beside her was just as adept a politician but was a little blunter or perhaps had a little less patience today.

'Yes it is.' Bevan's voice was not loud, but it was forceful. 'Ellen's right this is a chance for you to fight back.'

The reply was equally powerful. 'We can get a better deal from Baldwin.'

The meeting was rapidly spiralling out of control; decades of mistrust and hatred were still standing between them.

It was time for Wilkinson to try a different approach. She stood up, her chair scraping on the gritty floor. 'No you won't get a better deal.' She forced an even brighter smile on her face. 'Yes Baldwin is privately sympathetic, how could he not be given his background? And yes, he's concerned about the balance of payments, but if you think he can deliver a steel tariff of fifty per cent for a year you're mistaken.'

'And if he can't', commented Bevan with sombre glee 'All the big shipyards will continue to close down every small yard they can and use the remaining ones to build ships with cheap foreign steel.'

He paused, and his face took on an expression of concern.

'And don't think that idea hasn't been whispered into the ears of certain ministers either. So Ellen's right, Baldwin can't deliver a better deal. Oh I grant you on paper he's got the numbers to force your tariff through if he gets the Liberals on side but that's not certain at all.' He grunted decisively and looked at Wilkinson, who picked up the baton.

'If Baldwin can't get the Liberal's to vote with him, then he'd have to make it a matter of confidence in the government', she explained, 'He won't want to do that too often, because it makes him look weak, and he may think that you are too minor a problem to risk his government on. What's more likely to happen is that he will delay forcing the issue if he doesn't think he has the numbers. Most likely he'll bury the issue in a select committee. It could take months.'

For a moment Wilkinson thought that they'd overplayed their hand, but a look at the grey faces opposite disproved that notion.

'So you see gentleman', she pleaded, 'We do have things in common, jobs are at risk, yours and those of Mr Bevan's union members. What we offer is certainty. With us you will see a market for your steel and you will see foreign steel attract a massive import duty.'

One of the grey faces swallowed his whiskey in a last convulsive gulp and asked the question they had been waiting to hear.

'Exactly how would this work?'

'Oh that's simple; Wilkinson said brightly, 'We want you to buy Palmers yards in Jarrow.'

The single light bulb which hung from a frayed cord in the ceiling didn't put out much light but was sufficient to throw into sharp relief the shock on the assembled faces.

Finally one of the faces summoned up sufficient strength to speak.

'Impossible.'

And there for a moment the matter stood, both parties seeming unable to move.

The spell was broken by the door opening, revealing a tall spindly barmaid who silently collected glasses and refreshed drinks. The door closed behind her shutting out the sounds of revelry and an out of tune piano.

The word was spoken again, though this time with just a hint of doubt which Bevan seized on. 'No not impossible, difficult yes but not impossible. Like Ellen said this is your chance to break free. Look, Baldwin won't like it. The big ship builders give a lot to Tory party funds and....'

'It won't come to that!'

Bevan only half succeeded in masking the look of scorn that fought to mould his face.

'Of course it will. It always has, and it always will. If it didn't you wouldn't be here tonight.'

He paused and took a long pull at what the barmaid assured him was their best tea. *She was wrong*, he thought and put down the cup without regret. 'You've asked Baldwin for a Tariff on imported steel. Fifty percent for a year. All the big ship builders, ship owners too for that matter, will scream bloody murder over the idea. Already are of course. His heart may want to help you, but the shipbuilders have a very loud voice and it reaches into a lot of places. Baldwin has to consider his own party as well as Westminster. I'm sure he's had a few discreet visits from influential Tories already. And like I said he may not have the numbers to do as wishes.'

'You've placed him in a bad position, a very bad position', Wilkinson explained gently, 'His instinct will be to bury the whole idea in a select committee so that any blame can be shared.'

Bevan reached out for his cup and then thought better of it. 'And we sit on those committees, sometimes they can sit for weeks on end, months even.'

Ernest Bevan was a huge, physically imposing man but his voice was quiet, almost bland and though it held no hint of menace, the threat was very evident. He decided to make sure that threat was plainly understood.

'My union and others are opposed to tariffs, besides which it happens to be Labour party policy to oppose them. Now if, just supposing Baldwin puts the idea to a committee, which it's likely he will, then it would be our plain duty to make sure that your request is delayed. Oh you'll get some sort of tariff eventually, but how many of you will be left? Better to get what you can get quickly.'

Now the threat was out in the open Wilkinson saw her way back into the conversation. 'But it needn't come to that if you offer a compromise. You tell the government that though you want fifty per cent you will accept forty if you are allowed to buy Palmers in Jarrow, and if Palmers is given a government contract. The big ship builders don't want your steel? Fine. Sell it to yourself. Forty percent tariff and an assured income gives you a chance to breathe again and you need that.'

Bevan pushed his tea cup away from him knowing that Wilkinson was fighting for her electorate and he could trust her on this issue. He stood up for a moment stretching tense muscles and then spoke. 'Best of all though is that Baldwin can sell the idea to everyone. He can tell the shipbuilders that he beat you down, he can tell the public that the government is open to new ideas and job creation and he can show foreign governments that he's not willing to accept steel dumping.'

One steel man had remained in the background listening very intently. He took off his glasses and carefully polished them on a spotless handkerchief. 'Not as easy as that though is it? Firstly Palmers yard is under a covenant; you can't build so much as a rowing boat there for the next twenty years. Changing that in the teeth of the ship builders will not be easy.

'Secondly buying Palmers will cost money, where will that come from?

'And thirdly we know nothing about ship building so how does buying a bankrupt firm that we don't know how to run help us?

'Lastly if the government does not have the numbers or the nerve to pass a new tariff bill where will it find them to pass your amended proposal which as you say goes against your party's principles?'

He put his glasses back on with a determined air, sure that he had asked unanswerable questions.

Bevan grunted at the man acknowledging the sense of the questions. 'Ellen would you like to explain?'

Wilkinson grinned. They hadn't convinced these men, but at least they were talking.

'Alright', she began. 'Forcing a sale of Palmers and lifting the covenant will not be easy but remember the alternative the ship

51

builders face is a possible increase in basic costs. They are under pressure also, if nothing else the government will not be impressed if they become obstinate when with a little flexibility they can save them a good deal of trouble. As to the money you have been paying down debt for the past two years, and if all goes well you'll have a guaranteed income. Frankly I can't see your bankers refusing you.

'And you're right; you don't know anything about shipbuilding, but if you buy Palmers you have Jarrow, and if Jarrow knows one thing it's ship building. But your big concern is where does Baldwin get the numbers from?' She paused hoping that it would have the right effect.

'From us, Baldwin will get his support from us.'

Wilkinson kept her voice soft almost conspiratorial avoiding any dramatic tones. This was the moment, this was the moment that the whole scheme pivoted on. Could she convince them, could she prove her worth not just as an organiser, but as a negotiator? Could she win here, achieve victory not just for herself, but for Jarrow? She knew Bevan trusted her only so far, he would trust here where he could see her, where their interests aligned. But if she succeeded here his distrust would fade and even it didn't she would build her success into an unassailable powerbase. If she succeeded here Jarrow would be hers for decades to come. So she chose her words with care.

'Our judgement is that not only will you get a better deal by working with us, it's the only deal that Baldwin can easily get. If he had a big majority then we wouldn't be talking tonight, but he hasn't. We ran him too close in the election. He's beaten off one attack on his leadership already and there will be others you can be sure of that. He can't be sure of being able to persuade his rebels to back him without giving them more power and he's nervous about asking the Liberals; he may need their backing in a real crisis, but the more he asks the higher their price becomes. So if we just, on this one issue offer our help, believe me he'll see it as a way to avoid a crisis.'

She still kept her voice low and avoided any grand sweeping gestures. Had she convinced them, she wondered, had they bought her performance as a new M.P concerned for her constituency? Had Bevan proved to them that that his only concern was the welfare of his members? Looking at them she thought she had. It all sounded so plausible, and these men wanted to believe. Which made their task that much easier.

Except one man was only half convinced.

The glasses, already scrupulously clean were rubbed again and he irritably shuffled papers. 'Your price is still too high. We pay good money to buy a bankrupt ship yard, making you look like a guardian angel, and at the same time making Mr Bevan's position all but unassailable. But in return you expect us to accept two members of your union onto our board.'

Bevan's voice was like water running over boulders, melodious, but with unrevealed power. He looked across the cold tea into the eyes of the man. 'What do you suggest?'

The glasses were replaced, and a slow smile spread across his face. Wilkinson thought that he looked like a man who was suddenly sure he held a winning hand.

'One union member on Palmers new board and we still want a fifty percent tariff on foreign steel.'

Her diaphragm ceased flexing and she was sure her heart stopped in mid beat. This was so close to what they wanted.

Bevan paused, feigning deep but rapid thought. 'We'll ask for forty five percent, but you lose the right to veto our nomination.'

The man's smile broadened, and his resistance crumbled.

The next few hours were argument over details, clothing a body which had been born that night.

As Ellen Wilkinson walked back to her hotel the winter cold had no effect upon her, she glowed with happiness. No chill no matter how severe could remove the happiness she felt. The agreement hammered out tonight would benefit so many, but most of all it would help weaken an already fractured government.

And that of course was the real object of the night's exercise.

# BEGINNINGS

Yesterday was her birthday, a day of cake and kisses.

Most importantly it was the day when she was introduced to her new best friend. The doll was elegantly dressed and was obviously pleased to be with her. This last fact was obvious to her; if it was not so why did the doll have a permanent smile on her face?

As befitted a young woman who had entered her fourth year Isabella was most protective of her friend. She made sure that that she had a good view of the street below as they sat with Mamma watching the mid-day street traffic.

Mamma seemed a little odd today constantly looking down the street as if she was expecting Papa to come home early. Or perhaps she was sad because she did not have a new best friend? It was all very confusing, so she concentrated on trying to introduce her friend to the delights of taking afternoon coffee from the tiny tea set that lay scattered on the balcony. Strangely her friend seemed unwilling to participate in the occasion, though the smile never left her face.

She frowned concentrating harder and so missed the angry buzzing which erupted from a side street and flowed into the square. It was a church parade she thought, soon the Statue of the Virgin would appear, and older girls would throw flower petals in front of it. Secretly it was her ambition to perform such a task, so she leaned forward to get a better view.

It was not a church parade she saw. Placards had replaced petals and angry chants filled the air. Then just as the chants reached full volume another group of men started to object and began to sing different songs. Maybe, she thought they didn't like the first songs, they weren't like the ones Mamma sang to her so that was understandable.

Then it began to be horrible, both groups began hitting each other which was wrong. Mamma always said hitting people was wrong.

She began crying and her mother snatched her up and took her inside gently rocking her, seeking as mothers have always done to comfort their children.

She looked down at her new friend; the smile was plain and unmistakable on the face. She took comfort from it and her sobs gradually ceased, after all if her friend was not afraid why should she be? It was only when she looked at her mother's face that a little of her fear returned.


Georg Maikranz looked at the collection of iron and steel that was accumulating in front of his stores. It wasn't a ship, it wasn't even the parts of a ship, but one day with time and skill this collection of good German plate and girder would transform itself into a multi armed giant. A giant that would be the envy of all other navies, a giant that could crush all possible rivals.

And though he was a German patriot Georg hoped with all his heart that it would never be used. He hated war and had good reason for that hate. Four years in trenches had confirmed his patriotism, and he'd ended the war as a sergeant. He could have risen further, God knows towards the end any damn fool could become an officer.

But there was blight on his record, a blight that he had no regrets over. He'd saved a man's life, maybe two he wasn't sure.

He often thought about that night in 1916.

He was cold he remembered, and a thin chilling rain was falling. They'd beaten off another British attack. As usual the Tommies had advanced with suicidal courage into massed machine gun fire.

And that night was filled with men. Appalled men, men that were sickened by slaughter, dead men and wounded men. One wounded man in particular. He was hung up on the wire, trapped in its folds, a soft groan forced from him at odd intervals.

They could do nothing, daylight might bring a temporary truce, then again it might not. It was academic in any case; wounds and exposure would undoubtedly finish him off before the sun rose. They hardened themselves to the sounds and so they missed the first sharp tinkling of the alarm bells. Someone was out there trying to rescue the wounded man.

It wasn't an attack; the sounds only came from one point so everyone relaxed.

It was live and let live at times like this and no one wished the rescuer anything but good luck.

Then some damn fool let off a flare and gave the order to fire. Something in Georg snapped and though he fired, he fired wide.

Others, though not all, followed his example and the rescuer with the wounded man slung over his shoulder escaped. It was a moment of humanity that stood out amongst other much less pleasant memories.

Naturally, there were consequences. He only just escaped a firing squad. As it was it took a year and a savage casualty rate for him to regain his previous rank.

Then there were the bitter years; defeat followed by rioting and political unrest, followed by financial collapse, followed by massive unemployment. Georg had suffered, all Germany had suffered until his country's genius for order re-exerted itself.

He was no supporter of the Nazi's, still less the Bolsheviks, but he had to admit that he lived in a stronger nation today and the collection of steel in front of him was evidence of that. His son would surely approve.

His son was a Nazi and had joined the Kriegsmarine last July on his fourteenth birthday. Though he was proud of his son he wished that his views were not so extreme.

He sighed and shook off his memories. Today not yesterday was important. He picked up his clip board and began to check the latest delivery. 'Alles ist in Ordnung' was his personal motto and he had no intention of deviating from it even by so much as a millimetre. When the ship builders came for their steel they would find him ready.


Spring had come to Chequers, replacing winters harsh hand with gentle caresses and cleansing rain. It would be a good day Baldwin thought to take a walk and let the cares of office fall from his shoulders. The rain might wash some of the ever-thickening fog which filled his head these days.

There was he realised little chance of that happening today or on any other day in the future. There were too many papers on his desk, reports and pleas, folders and envelopes, each and every one of them requiring an answer. He sighed, his mind struggling to comprehend the sheer number and complexity of them.

He picked up a folder at random and read a report issued from Madrid only a week ago.

Spain had taken more steps into anarchy; the British ambassador had requested an increased naval presence in Spanish waters and the formulation of plans for some sort of naval blockade in the event of civil war. The Navy, with what he thought was malicious glee had replied that it did not have the resources to even think of attempting such an exercise; indeed it was actually thinking of reducing its presence in the Mediterranean.

The reply from the Foreign Office was predictably apoplectic. It pointed out the disturbing interest Germany and Italy were taking in Spain, it lamented that with France in the process of forming yet another new government no cohesive joint policy could be expected for the next few months. It demanded an increased naval presence and suggested that in the event of civil war Germany and Italy should be 'encouraged' not to become involved.

He knew without reading it the response from the Admiralty. The Navy would use the crisis to press for more money; from their point of view the timing could not have been more perfect. The Naval estimates were due to be debated soon and that bled into another problem which he needed to decide upon.

The second folder was an offer, a very dangerous, and yet so very tempting offer. Potentially it solved not only his immediate problems, but the longer-term issues which were beginning to erode his power. Three by-elections in as many months was unfortunate but the dice had rolled that way and he had lost two out of the three. The reverberations from Labour's election campaign were still echoing, amending the accepted convention that new governments rarely lost by-elections in safe seats. The third by-election he had won, though with a reduced majority; hardly a ringing endorsement of his leadership.

And that was the problem; an even thinner majority made his job even more difficult. He could cope, but his back benchers had become restive. They had visions of the government withering away and having to deal with another general election. Not something they faced with relish, and as was usual in these cases the troops blamed the leadership.

Specifically him.

Already his web had detected the first stirrings of yet another revolt against him. There would be others; there always were and always would be, but it would become increasingly difficult to defeat them if his leadership was perceived as weak.

Labour's offer was a single issue one, but were they testing the water here; could he form a new coalition with the party which came so close to gaining power? If that was their motivation, if the pain of losing had pushed them to make this first tentative step then he could gain renewed power, and the rebels within his own party would shrink back into insignificance.

He could handle Attlee he was sure, but what of his own people? Would they swallow their hatred and distaste and vote with the enemy? Would they accept this alliance?

The alternative was a government potentially bleeding to death over the life time of this Parliament however long that might be. There were too many questions and realistically only one way to find out.


It was undoubtedly a good cigar; the man smoking was unlikely to smoke an inferior brand. In all the years Roger Keyes had known the man, in all the years of triumph and tragedy, of scandal and success the cigar had never varied and was the most obvious of his habits. Though it had a close rival in expensive brandy.

Someone had once described the man as having the face of a particularly naughty cherub, and that was a very apt description, though tonight what they were planning had more to do with hell than heaven.

The cigar flared a deep red as the smoke from Cuba's finest product was drawn into lungs long since hardened to the abuse.

'It won't do, it simply won't do.' The cigar was now performing its secondary function as a punctuation device. Each word was accompanied by a savage stab of the air which left smoky hieroglyphics of aromatic vapour floating lazily in the air.

Keyes waited, from long experience he knew that his friend would get to the point in his own time. He had heard the rumours and wanted to know just what the MP for Epping thought of them.

'It won't do Keyes, these people are the enemy, not just opponents.

And if Baldwin even considers entering into some sort of pact with Attlee it will be our sad but plain duty to remove him from office.' A half grin was visible through the rings of smoke and brandy fumes. 'That is of course if he is stupid enough to take up the offer.'

Keyes was not convinced. 'If there is an offer.'

The grin broadened. 'Oh there's an offer, a quiet whispered offer; I can feel it. Anyway rumours come and go in our business - we both know that - but this one has come and stayed. And it's done more than stay, it's grown. Even the newspapers have begun to pick up on the rumours. The Labour party has offered itself as a stick to beat us. Baldwin thinks he will have a new grasp on power and a means to firmly close the lid on us. But it's a backdoor into government for Labour where they get all the pleasure and none of the pain.'

Keyes took his role as devil's advocate seriously, so he sought to pierce his friend's arguments. 'As I understand the rumour merely involves one shipyard and one project, not something we can seriously object to. After all haven't we been arguing for just such a thing?'

The cigar glowed again. 'It's the principle that matters, and besides do you seriously think Attlee wants us to rearm? Of course not, and even if he does he's not established himself in the party to over- ride the pacifists. He'll pick and choose just which causes to back and Baldwin will be thrown back on his agreement with the Liberals. Oh Baldwin can use them to push us back, but what if it's not just us that he uses them on, that's the line to take. Our party has many strands,; if one can be molested so can they all.'

Keyes was still not convinced. 'So we use this to topple Baldwin and you become PM?'

The cigar was dismissive. 'My dear Keyes I'm touched by your support truly I am, but realistically it has to be Chamberlain. I am too divisive a figure.'

'Not Duff Cooper then?'

'Ah he would be Baldwin's choice for successor, but he's seen as Baldwin's man and that will tell against him I think. No, my money's on Chamberlain.'

'He's an accountant! The man has the personality of a lump of driftwood!'

A great cloud of blue smoke hid the chuckle and didn't disguise the small element of gleeful agreement. 'Oh I agree, and yet that may be just what the Party needs, and as his strength is most decidedly not on foreign affairs, still less on defence matters this aids our own particular cause a great deal I would imagine.'

Keyes was intrigued. 'So we drop a few choice remarks amongst your fellow back benchers and Chamberlain benefits ...if he's smart enough.'

'My dear Keyes the man may be dry as dust, but I have never underestimated his intelligence. Mark my words once he sees which way the wind is blowing he'll trim his sails accordingly. And as Duff Cooper and his followers hate Chamberlain with vitriolic passion I believe that with a small amount of effort they can be persuaded to align themselves with our merry band.'

The cigar took a last self-satisfied glow and was discarded. And a large brandy took its place.

Keyes was only half convinced; his mercurial friend often had these semi –plausible ideas which swiftly arrived and as swiftly departed.

'So we sow discontent in the ranks and follow Chamberlain into power ...if he lets us, but what do we do about the Labour proposal for the shipyard? It's bound to come up in the Naval estimates debate, do we back Baldwin and let Labour off the hook? We can't oppose what amounts to new capacity, it's what we've argued in favour of for all these years.'

The brandy fumes rolled forward not blurring the reply at all. 'Of course we back naval construction but we do it our way. Here's what we do.'

As the plan unfolded Keyes began to smile and then laugh just a little. 'That really is a clever idea, you know.'

The cherub smiled back at him. 'It is.' Winston Churchill's smile morphed into a sardonic grin. 'And best of all Roger you gave me the idea.'


Her friend the doll was still smiling when the soldiers came.

They were sitting at the cafe with Aunt Theresa enjoying the sunshine and she was trying to explain to her aunt all about her new adventures with her friend, but she was not certain that her aunt was listening. Perhaps it was because she was missing Uncle Vicente. He was always funny and when he kissed her his beard tickled her and made her laugh.

Yes, she decided that must be it that her aunt was missing Uncle Vicente and being tickled by his beard. Certainly when Papa had brought her back from the railway station she was crying so that must be it. Having settled the matter in her mind she raised up her little friend so that she could get a better view of the soldiers as they marched into the square.

The soldiers were very serious and were not smiling at all as they began to paste up little pieces of paper on the walls of houses. One of them made a small speech and set up a small table and chair. Some of the soldiers dragged Senor Rosario from his shop and took him to the soldier with the table. The soldier looked at a list, spoke a few words to Senor Rosario and then pointed down the street. Senor Rosario was taken away and she wondered how Mama would do her shopping now that he was not there to serve her. It was all very strange, but her friend was still smiling so she was not afraid.

But what had Aunt Theresa meant when she had told Mamma; "Oh Sophia, it's happening here too?"

The two apprentices were the same age as his son and stood rather nervously in his office while he carefully scanned the requisition.

Though he could see that the form had been correctly completed he had a reputation to maintain and it would not do to show any signs of haste or slackness.

'Fourteen pieces of twenty -millimetre sheet and eleven meters of rolled beam.' He looked up from the paper and gazed at the boys who were so like his son. 'Well everything is in order here.' A great rubber stamp flashed down and he affixed a neat signature to the form.

The boys relaxed a little, Herr Maikranz was well known to be a stickler for order, a man of absolute devotion to duty and few words, so they were surprised when he un-stiffened a little and engaged them in conversation. 'What are you building boys?'

The taller of the two apprentices hid his surprise and answered. 'We are from the sub assembly shed. We are building the hatch for turret Anton.'

Georg nodded approvingly.

'It is important work, do it well for yourselves and for Germany, remember what you build today must pass not only the inspector's eye but that of the German people. Many German sailors must pass through that hatch make sure that they do so with pride. Learn and learn well and little harm will come to you. Now take your requisition to the storeman and your steel will be given to you. Good luck gentlemen.'

As the two boys left Georg reflected that he wished his own son had taken a similar path instead of joining the Kriegsmarine. To fight for Germany had been his sons wish and his father's tales of death and suffering had not quenched that desire or altered his convictions at all. Georg had tried, God himself knew that he had tried. He had raged and shouted while his wife had shed bitter tears but against the Fuehrer's words they had counted for little.

And so he hoped for peace. He was building a mighty warship and yet he still hoped for peace.

There was little glory in war despite what his son may think. And who would know that better than he?

The Palace of Westminster showed an uneven face to the world at this time of the morning. Some windows were dark voids; empty of all but papers and problems deemed too insignificant or too troublesome to waste sleep on. Others blazed with light as the diligent or the ambitious, burnt their energy on events the importance which only Dame History could judge.

Clement Attlee was tired but was reviewing past events trying to find alternative paths that could have been taken. Hoping that the mistakes of the past could give birth to the successes of the future. Had he been victorious, or had he been defeated? He could not decide.

Had his opponents suffered, or were they organised in such a way as to make the terms meaningless?

The difference between his party and the one that Baldwin led was that of leadership. He was content to allow every strand of opinion within the Labour party to share power whereas several shades of opinion that Baldwin found inconvenient were side lined in favour of those whose outlook was less challenging.

He understood the problem of course. Running a coalition government meant sharing power at the expense of a very vocal group of MPs.

The divisions between them had been allowed to deepen and fissure. And the Labour Party's limited offer of support for Baldwin had been designed from the start to probe those fissures. He'd gambled that Baldwin would not be able to resist the temptation laid before him and would hope that this was an opening move into a semi-formal coalition. He'd gambled and had come very close to total victory, but at last, just as the scents and flavours of winning had become real to him full victory had been denied him.

This past month had been bloody; very, very bloody.

Convincing the cabinet even without the manacles of collective responsibility had proved impossible and Baldwin had entered the floor of the House of Commons looking supremely confident, but without the backing of some of his cabinet.

It soon became apparent just why he was so supremely confident.

With Labour support the Steel Tariff was approved and the legislation to allow the sale of Palmers and permission to bid for government contracts was passed despite vociferous opposition.

Despite the rumours the shock in the House was palpable. Labour's reversal of policy had given Baldwin a new source of strength and a new way of enforcing his will. Baldwin's rebels had been vanquished and the master helmsman had once more steered away from the rocks. Or so it seemed.

For a few days Parliament was subdued; no one knew the extent of Baldwin's new power. Did it run deep or shallow? Was the flow constant or did it wax and wane? Rumour after rumour swept through the Gothic revival building like errant and opposing tides.

And although each rumour seemed plausible the truth was that no one knew for certain. The only real truth was that political certainties were based on numbers and now the numbers, the true numbers were hidden.

On the day when the Navy estimates were due to be debated no one was expecting any surprises. The bill was a money bill and therefore covered by Baldwin's paper-thin confidence and supply agreement with the Liberals. There would be no shocks this day, no staggering alarms, nothing out of the ordinary. This would be an ordinary day like the great majority of days in Westminster; the exact figures for the estimates had been long since calculated down to the last penny.

There was agreement.

All was proceeding well until they were ambushed by Churchill.

With a very grave voice he asked, when the navy estimates were already unfeasibly low how the Navy was supposed to support another ship yard. He applauded the initiative but pointed out that the estimates were made long before Palmers was even considered as a new source of naval construction. He spoke for but a few short moments before delivering his final lines, which indicated that unless the estimates were revised upwards he would not support their passage through the House. The words were sparks on dry tinder; the newspapers had been filled with tales of how the Navy was planning further cutbacks.

The debate was fierce.

The opponents of re- armament baying for blood, while Churchill fought with facts the government wished to remain hidden. Two battleships to be mothballed, bases closed, recruitment cut.

His opponents fought back but it was too late, the damage had been done. Churchill led a small group of diehard backbenchers, but although they were a small group they were large enough to defeat Baldwin's reduced majority, and he and everyone else knew it.

What should have been a gentle passage for an innocuous bill had become a challenge, both for the government and for him. Churchill had trapped not only Baldwin but had threatened his own carefully crafted scheme. It may not have been a defeat, but it was far from victory.

And all he could do; all Baldwin could do was wait and see what price Churchill would demand.

Wait.

And hope.

The smile was never far from Churchill's face. He believed it to be the smile of victory. Could he call it victory? Churchill was absolutely certain that they could; others were not so sure, but he knew victory when he saw it.

The ambush had been perfect, the ground for it perfectly prepared, perfectly tilled and harrowed. His friends, those that were committed to the cause had done their job well. Rumour had joined conjecture in un-holy matrimony and given birth to tenuous truths. Truths that were designed to bring forth a rich crop of discord.

It took just a few hundred words to trap the Prime minister and to force Attlee to choose between three equally unpalatable futures.

He could abandon Baldwin, losing the back door to power but appeasing those in his party who believed in disarmament and the League of Nations, or he could support Baldwin; keeping open the door, but then endangering his own position within his party by seeming to repeat the mistakes of Ramsey MacDonald by becoming too subservient to the hated Tories.

Of course Attlee could back those who believed his country should speak with a louder voice, but that option he dismissed without further thought.

No, unless he was mistaken Attlee's whole scheme was designed from the outset to weaken Baldwin, ultimately; he did not care about steel manufacturers, ship yards or depressed towns. His one object was to remove Baldwin.

He'd let both men simmer in their own juices for the weekend and then reach out. Because although they were enemies, ultimately both he and Attlee had the same objective.


Ellen Wilkinson drew deeply on the cigarette pulling the soothing smoke deep into her lungs.

Was it victory?

She wasn't sure. It was a victory for her, of that much she was certain.

After Churchill's shock announcement Roger Keyes had stood in Parliament and taken on the unlikely role of peacemaker. He proposed that Palmers shipyards should be given not a contract for a new ship, but only a refurbishment of an existing ship. This had taken much of the ire from the mouths of the ship builders federation and his second proposal that the cost of one of the rebuilds should be borne by the issue of government bonds specifically issued for that purpose had been seized upon by both Baldwin and her leader as a way out of the trap Churchill had laid for them.

In that sense both men had lost, and Churchill had won, as the Navy had gained an effective increase in funding. Which she rather suspected was one of Churchills objectives in any case.

And there were other losers as well of course. The Foreign Office was appalled at just how such a bond issue would be received in Berlin, Rome and Tokyo. The Exchequer had now been burdened with an extra cost although it could console itself with the thought that payment would not be demanded for another twenty years. Chamberlain was said to be furious that his concerns over the allocation of funds had been ignored and was considering resignation.

It was strange she thought that out of all the anger and drama of the past month the two biggest winners should be her and Churchill, the north and south of the political magnet.

She stubbed out her cigarette and put on her coat.

There was much to do today. For the Labour Party...and for Jarrow.


Baldwin sat in the over-stuffed chair and let the fatigue wash over him. He'd survived.

Survived in the same way a wounded Buffalo survived an attack by wolves. Bleeding. Staggering. But alive.

Was this victory?

He'd beaten his enemies, but they still lived and breathed. He'd gained allies, but they weren't dependable. He'd lost friends and they weren't replaceable. But this was victory.

Wasn't it?

# RETURN

It was the wave that woke the Hood.

The wave had been born in an Atlantic gale fierce and wild, brothers and sisters she had in uncountable numbers, but time and tide had worn them into weak and worthless swells, unworthy of the storm that sired them.

The wave was an orphan, her parent had long since scattered into a dozen harmless zephyrs and a thousand rainclouds. It alone was the sole inheritor of long-lost power. The wave had run swift and strong from Cape Hatteras and was now surging barely diminished down the English Channel.

The, rust stained ship could offer no resistance and lifted first a battered and patched stern and then the proud knife edged bow. Spray, cold and wet broke over her giving birth to a hundred salt laden rainbows.

The shock was enough to wake her from her long sleep.

She'd dreamt. Long confusing, horrifying dreams. Of death and defeat. Of failure and oblivion. She shook herself as water drained from her scuppers. Such dreams were nonsense. She was what she was, and no ship afloat would dare challenge her.

She was moving she was certain of that; the salt air blew through her upper works in a manner which triggered memories of other days. But her crew, the ever-changing mix of men and boys who gave meaning to her life were missing. A few men wandered within her, but they were strangers, not friends. So why was she moving when her engines did not beat, nor her propellers turn?

It was still puzzling her as she was pulled through the Channel and into the North Sea.


Life had taught Geordie McIntyre patience. Four years in the trenches had reinforced the lesson and it had served him well in the years after.

He was patient on his long march.

He was patient while the shipyard was re-born, and dredgers re-dug a channel in the river.

Today though patience had surrendered to frustration and he strained his eyes trying to see through the fog to where salvation lay.

Except salvation was late.

So he and thousands of others stood on the dockyard and waited. Men and women, young and old, tall and straight or bent with age they stood in silence, only the forlorn cry of gulls navigating their way through the fog was heard. They waited until the sun, ruler of all things had at long last decided to reassert his mastery. He put forth his arms and the fog recoiled from their supremacy. Drop by drop, strand by strand it vanished and at long last Geordie and his friends saw their salvation.

She was rusty but even at a distance her beauty was apparent. She was Geordie thought the most beautiful thing he had ever seen.

There was no cheering, the excitement, the relief would not be sullied by that, but there was an excited buzz as the Hood turned down the newly dredged channel.

Finally at long last the fog had lifted from the Tyne. And Geordie's patience was at long last rewarded.


Blindly she could only trust in the tiny ships that had pulled her through the brackish water. She could still hear and feel. Mournful blasts of steam from her tugs which she was powerless to echo. The slap of waves against her sides which she was unable to resist. The frustration which had been building for days began to surge through her, every rivet, every plate vibrated with her anger. She would protest, she was a warrior, and this was undignified.

It was only as the fog lifted that her anger abated and at last she understood. She had come home.

At last.


It was still dark when Geordie woke, the old habits gripping once more. To rise early was a natural thing, a comforting thing of memory and joy. Yet early as he rose Mabel had risen before him. The kettle hissed with excitement and a single lamp illuminated a sparse breakfast. He ate with speed, for the day awaited. A quick kiss from Mabel and he pulled the door behind him, joining others as they walked down the rain slicked cobbled street.

Towards the Hood. Towards work.


She felt secure and yet at the same time naked.

The men who swarmed through her were friends she was certain of that. And yet she puzzled over what they were doing to her. Distant memories of her birth were triggered, but this was not a birth. This time there was no gradual recognition that she was, no moment that she became a ship, an idea, a force. No, this was different; this was strange, not frightening, but still unsettling. There was no sense that this was death, but if she had found a home what was happening to her?

She quivered a little as a piece of her was ripped from her side.

She came to a decision. A good warrior was patient, only a fool rushed into fear and she was an old warrior tested and true. She would wait and while she waited she would absorb.

Every emotion that her friends felt would now become part of her.

Every victory, every difficulty she would take up and accept.

Every bit of pain, every drop of sweat would become part of her, would make her stronger, more determined.

For she was the Hood.

And she would live.


The flame was an intense blue white that cut with disdainful ease through the last bolt.

With the skill born of long practice Geordie smashed the still glowing bolt and the plate swung away with a wrench that was only arrested by the chains that linked the plate to the massive overhead crane. He stepped back and made a curious whirling motion with his right hand.

Far above him and with surprising delicacy the crane lifted the armour plate and delivered it with barely a scratch to the growing pile on the side of the dock.

To build and build well it was first necessary to destroy. Once that was done then the Hood would begin to grow. New engines which would be her hearts and new propellers to push her through the water swifter than ever. A new stern and a raised deck over it to keep at bay the sea. Unseen bulges to force the sea to do her bidding and defeat the strike of the torpedo. A new superstructure and bridge where those whose duty it was to guide her could do so in comfort and safety.

Her guns which could fire tons of death would move swifter than ever, pushed by more modern motors. New smaller guns which would destroy with ease any little ships that were foolish enough to tempt her anger. New bulkheads to replace those that time and experience had shown were badly placed or unwanted. A thousand or more tiny details.

Much that was deemed unnecessary would be removed, never to be reinstalled. She would be re-floated and her armour or at least most of it would be refitted.

Geordie didn't pretend to understand why his would be done, he knew steel and how to shape it, but he placed his faith in the men in the offices. It was they who had decided that the old armour would be used, redistributed to be sure but she would still be wearing the same clothes as when she arrived. Only the deck armour would be new; thicker or thinner as the potential danger compelled.

All this had been explained to him, they had shown him the picture of what many months from now his saviour would look like. The artist had done a good job; the Hood was shown thrusting through the water freshly painted looking sleek and very menacing.

But there was much hard work to be done between now and that day. There was another plate to remove and he reached up to pull down his goggles. As he did so a tiny drop of sweat fell from his brow and fell un- noticed into the bowels of the ship.

It accelerated down splashing into a million atoms.

The Hood accepted it gratefully, absorbing not only the salty water but the feelings and emotions that went with it.

Without realising it, without ever knowing it Geordie and the Hood were now joined.

70

The stranger lay on the table mute and uncompromising.

Geordie had left it there this morning and there it had lain...... untouched.

Mabel deliberately busied herself, dusting the already dusted and tidying the already perfect. She straightened the picture of her husband with the Prince of Wales and polished the tarnished surface of the dining table. And yet throughout the morning the stranger never moved and always her eyes were drawn to it as if it had some awful power over her.

Her hand had stretched out a dozen times but each time she stopped, half believing that if she made contact with the stranger it would vanish taking her hopes with it.

Finally she could resist no longer, and her fingers closed around the plain brown envelope tearing open the flap which offered only minimal resistance.

Two used bank notes were inside along with a handful of coins. Geordie's first pay packet had arrived.

She sat staring at the money for what seemed an age while the emotions swirled inside her.

And then she burst into tears.

# RISING POWERS

Franz Maikranz had chosen the postcard with care

The gaudy and the colourful would not appeal, so he chose a tasteful scene of flamenco dancers. He knew his mother would enjoy the post card and it would be shown to each and every neighbour. He could see her now boasting of her son the sailor who was helping people in far- away lands.

He smiled a little at the scene and then the smile faded as he thought that his father would also see the card. He knew the man would dismiss the scene as being far too exuberant, for his father distrusted extremes and the passion the dancers showed would not appeal to him. Duty and a solid unwavering focus on whatever task lay in front of him were the two lodestones that ruled his life. He had no time for excessive emotion in life or in politics.

It was an attitude that had led to their last and greatest quarrel.

Franz fervently believed in the Fuhrer, a man his father believed to be unbalanced. He could not understand that to Franz Adolf Hitler was the saviour of Germany and all she stood for.

The quarrel grew and grew, without either side wanting the battle or knowing how to end it. It festered between them, truce after truce broken, until despairing of ever finding peace or convincing his father he had joined the Navy and was now a very humble junior rating on a tiny gunboat that was part of Germany's contribution to the international flotilla that sought to cordon a waring Spain.

He straightened his back and dipped the pen in the ink pot, he must be careful in writing, his words must console his mother and pacify his father.

It was a difficult task for so young a boy.

Cold bratwurst, coleslaw and hard bread was not much of a meal, but Georg Maikranz was content enough; he'd eaten far worse in the trenches and only a few years ago he'd eaten far less for what little food he did have went on his family. This was not a thing that he had done consciously, to eat when his family was still hungry would be unnatural and he'd never even considered it as an option. But those days were past and though it seemed unlikely that he would ever dine at a fancy restaurant he ate well enough.

Did he have the Fuhrer to thank for that?

Certainly, the Fuhrer claimed that he had rescued Germany and ever since the re occupation of the Rhineland the rhetoric had stepped up. The memory of 1923 was branded deep into Georg's memory as it was in every German and if he was honest he had rejoiced when he heard that his country had regained another of her borders. Time had proved the Fuhrer to be right…at least this time.

He swallowed the last of his coffee and picked up again the worn post postcard with the foreign postage stamp. It was a tasteful scene of Spanish flamenco dancers. George wasn't interested in the scenes of Spanish nightlife; he knew very well that his son had chosen the post card for his mother's benefit not his.

He read again the words he knew by heart. Assurances that all was well, there was no danger and the German flag was respected once more. He sensed the pride in his son's words and they forced him to ask a question that he was still unwilling to answer. Wasn't Germany's contribution to the Spanish naval blockade a sign that the Fuhrer's policies were right?

And if that was so then the steel giant that grew not far from his office was a visible sign of the success of those ideas. Was he wrong in dismissing the Fuhrer as a ranting fanatic?

He traced with a blunt forefinger the words his son had written hoping that in them he would find the answers to his questions. As he feared the answers failed to appear and he carefully placed the card back in his pocket, patting it gently into place.

He missed his son.


'A thousand pounds?'

The voice was incredulous and was loud enough to fill the council chamber.

'I would remind the mayor that many in this community are still without basic sanitation and that a thousand pounds would go a long way to providing clean water and decent sewerage to many that are suffering all the ills that accompany this lack. When I think…'

The voice stopped registering on David Riley's ears; it was only to be expected and it was best to allow the objections to be said before he replied. Finally the last of the red -faced objectors sat down, secure in the knowledge that they had dealt Riley's idea not one but several death blows.

He stood up, his great bulk rising from the chair like a suddenly released iceberg. 'It's time ' he said, 'Time we put our money where our mouth is'. His voice was soft and clear as he reminded them of the recent past. 'Did we not ask for work and fight for it, did I imagine street corner collections and jumble sales? Did I or did I not see every church plate passed round twice every Sunday for a solid month?' He paused and looked around the council chamber, great meaty hands gripping the lapels of his jacket.

He took a deep breath and bellowed out his next words. 'Did I imagine one man with the weight of a whole town on his shoulders marching to London and beyond to put food in our bellies? There's a bloody great ship in Palmer's dockyard today and its pumping more money into this town than we've seen in many a long year.

'Sewerage?' There was loud scorn in his voice now and a long thick finger swung round pointed at his chief detractor. 'Two years ago we were turning off the bloody street lights to save money we didn't have in the first place, that's how bad it was. Don't talk to me about bloody sewerage'.

The unexpected change in volume had washed over the council like a high wind in a wheat field and Riley knew that for now he had the advantage.

'We did all that and now we just sit back? Ask yourself this, what happens when the Hood leaves, when the pay-packets become thin and then stop, when men begin to hang around street corners again and the bairns cry. What do we do then, send another lone man walking mile after mile? That's a game that can be played only once, we were lucky last time, next time we may not be so lucky. So we act now, the Treasury is issuing bonds, government bonds at three per cent specifically to pay for the Hood. I say we buy some. Three per cent gentlemen, and in twenty-five years, in 1961 our sons get their thousand back and, in the meantime, we collect the interest. But the interest is not that important, what is important is that we lead so that others can follow.

'Jarrow has the Hood, but she doesn't have her all to herself; there's steel from Wales, brass from Birmingham, tin and lead from Cornwall, paint from Cheshire, a hundred towns and cities pour their skill into Jarrow. Palmer's gates are wide open every day and every day money flows out of them across the country, and if Jarrow dies again a few other towns die a little too.

'So we invest in ourselves and encourage other towns to invest as well as best they can. And then we can show the new owners of Palmer's that we stand behind them and behind us stand others, each and every one of them ready to help win new orders for Jarrow'.

He paused again to let his idea sink in to the collective mind of the council chamber; he had his supporters of course, men he could rely on, but he had his rivals, those that envied his success. Those men he would never convince, but there were others, those who were neutral or undecided, they were the ones that he needed to win over.

Riley, like every politician great or small was a consummate actor so he placed a beguiling smile on his face and put pleading humility in his mouth. 'Maybe I was wrong when I said Jarrow has the Hood. After all we are only borrowing her, but if we are clever we make her the people's ship, a ship that has links in every town that helps us. We build lasting ties with those ties, strong ties, ties that speak with one voice, act with one purpose. Then they won't dare let us die again. Then they will give us new ships and more work, so much work in fact that we can replace every dammed sewer in Jarrow and build new houses on top of them. A prosperous town filled with prosperous people, that's what I'm asking you to vote on today. A thousand pounds is a cheap price to pay for security.'

He looked around for the last time at the men who sat in the layered benches; each and every one of them he tried to look into their eyes, to make contact not with words but to allow a little of his love for Jarrow to flow into them.

The actor in him retreated and it was the real David Riley who asked one last question. 'Or do you want to go down as the men who let Jarrow die again?'

His bulk collapsed back into a chair which had long since become used to sudden strains. His eyes were now closed, not in pain or weariness, but to try and shut out the vision he had of Jarrow sliding back, of dead eyed men walking dead end streets. He hoped that his words were enough to persuade if not convince, but even if he lost todays battle it did not matter.

Because Jarrow had risen and would not fall again.

Of that he was quite certain.


All in all it was a magnificent speech. Every word, every sentence, every gesture had been designed not to cut or hurt, but to main and kill.

And Churchill had not raised a finger to help his leader.

Attlee's address had eviscerated a lacklustre Baldwin, and it was obvious that the Prime Minister was living the last moments of his political life.

Every occupant of Number Ten walked through the door holding a finite amount of political capital and Baldwin had little enough to begin with and recent events had reduced it still further. Simply put the Prime Minister no longer had the full confidence of his Party. Certainly, he did not have Churchill's support, nor the support of those he had gathered around him.

They were few.

But enough.

And when Baldwin fell as fall he must then Neville Chamberlain would rise to power and would be forced to include him in government.

A small grin lit his face. A place in Cabinet would be very nice after so many years in the wilderness.

He would be a disruptive influence in cabinet.

Of that he had no doubt.

Because that is what rising powers did.

# A SEA OF TROUBLES

It had been a tough few years for the S.S Isabel Anne and her owner. Work, once plentiful had become erratic and harder to find. Rates which once gave a good living had vanished, replaced by thin and meagre copies which had all but a tiny vestige of profit removed. His ship was all he had, all he was likely to have for that matter. Without her he was nothing, with her he was a captain; a man of substance, of respectability. He would not, could not abandon his ship and all it represented and so had begun the slow slide down.

Questions which once he would have asked now went unasked. Crewmen he once would have left on the dockside now filed his bunks. And worse still cargoes which a few years ago would have been considered an insane risk were now all that stood between him and disaster.

Which is why, in his holds covered by several tons of Irish potatoes lay four hundred rifles, once the gift of imperial Germany to Irish rebels.

There was nothing to worry about.

He would time his run to Spain so that he would dock in the early twilight. The guns would be unloaded and a large amount of cash would be placed in his hands.

He didn't care who would take the guns or why, the affairs of foreigners were no concern of his. His only concern was his bank balance and soon that would be healthier than it had been for some time.

Naturally if asked he would be delighted to make return journeys.

There really was nothing to worry about.


Turn to port.

Steam for one hundred and fifty miles.

Turn to port.

Turn and turn and turn.

Turn until tedium is not just a word but an ever-present ghost that sits unwanted in every mess and wardroom. Turn until every word spoken is a repeat of others equally mundane and every tick or idiosyncratic foible is an open insult begging for retribution. Turn until the sight of another ship or even rarer passage of a seabird is a thing of wonder.

Not even the captain knew why his and dozens of other ships were patrolling the waters off Spain. The politicians spoke of an international effort to blockade a Spain where civil war was more than a phrase, but a bloody reality faced every day. Starve those who fought of the weapons they needed, and the world could return to peaceful sleep. A theory preached by those who did not have to contend with a windswept Bay of Biscay, its barren waves and endless, endless patrolling.

A theory with too many unanswered questions.

Were they to aid British ships? No one knew.

Were they to fire upon Spanish ships if required? There was no answer.

Who was the legitimate Spanish government? There was only an embarrassed silence.

She was the Foxhound, one of newest destroyers in His Majesty's Navy, a lone ship exiled to sail a pointless path until someone, somewhere made a decision of just what to do about a war everybody expected and only a few wanted.

Turn to port.

Turn and turn and turn.

It was all so bloody pointless.


She was being pursued by a monster, a terrible grey painted monster. The monster wanted her to stop, but she could not, for only death awaited her if she did. So she dodged into rain storms, hoped that night would be her friend and prayed for a miracle. The dark was stabbed by bright beams of light as the monster pursued her through the late summer night. The Isabel Anne had pitted cunning, disguise and the vastness of the ocean against death and destruction.

Again and again she'd rolled the dice and the gods had smiled, amused at her audacity. Now the gods had turned their faces away from her. Now she was on her own and must make her own luck.

So her crew cursed as they fed her straining engines, engines that threw black smoke into a black moonless sky.

Her captain cursed as he steered, too frightened to look over his shoulder, promising that if he survived this night he would leave the sea forever and use his profits to buy a cottage far, far away from the coast.

Run.

Never look behind.

Run.

And the night swallowed her.


It was just before dawn when the Foxhound's captain arrived on the bridge. A cup of hot cocoa was placed in his hands and he drank deeply, grateful for the temporary warmth.

August in the Bay of Biscay was a deceitful month, it promised much but delivered its scanty cargo of sunshine fitfully. Today he decided was not going to be a day when the sun put his hat on and came out to play no matter what the song said.

Despite that the cocoa had done its work and he had a sense that nothing too concerning was going to happen today. He took in a deep draught of regretfully cold air and began the morning routine. 'Morning Osbourne anything to report?'

Osbourne turned bleary eyes on his captain. 'No sir, we saw lights at 03.39, but that was all.'

'Lights?' the captain was intrigued, 'Where away?'

Osbourne was not a night owl and could feel sleep growling impatiently, but habits long formed overrode mere bodily weakness. 'Fine on the starboard bow sir, the lookout thought they may be searchlights from a warship, but he couldn't be sure'. Sleep growled again, louder this time and more impatient than ever. 'Sir we're due to make our turn soon, do you wish me to give the order, or do you relieve me?'

Every good destroyer captain knew his men and he knew that Osbourne was renowned for his ability to sleep the clock round and was therefore now suffering agonies of sleep deprivation, so the question was answered with a wry grin and the formal words that transferred control of the ship.

Osbourne vanished as if he and his cot were the opposite poles of two newly powerful magnets.

The captain drew a deep breath and was about to give the orders which would turn the ship onto a new course when he paused.

Lights? Possibly search lights?

A few more minutes on this course could not hurt, it would be full light soon and he could get a better view of what was out there.

Probably nothing, but at least it broke the monotony.


Night had shielded the Isabel Ann, swept her up in his dark cloak, but now night was weakening, a resurgent day was leaching the blackness away replacing it with a thrice cursed sunrise. But the monster had not found her, his long fingers had not touched her sides and surely, she would live to see another day. Promises made during the night were now forgotten washed away by victorious exultation. Dreams of cottages and retirement slaughtered by wide eyed grins.

It was a single cry from the lookout that caused the joy to empty from them like water from an overturned jug.

The monster was back. Just on the horizon, a tiny speck no bigger than a grain of rice. As they looked it saw them, silhouetted against the rising sun. There was a moment's hesitation and then it turned a cruel edged bow.

All they could do was run.

Run towards the rising sun.


It had been full daylight now for over twenty minutes, and the long sharp-edged shadows that the fickle sun threw before them had begun to shrink and blur.

There was nothing.

No ships. Not even a hopelessly lost seagull. Only the eternal glassy green waves marching ever eastwards.

So much for Osbourne's lights. Whatever they were, whatever had caused them had gone, vanished into the desert of waves.

A little regretfully he gave the order and the ship began to turn onto her new course, completing another lap in an endless race.

Later, much later after the gold braid had deliberated, and the politicians and the journalists had dipped their oars into the whole bloody mess he wondered what would have happened if he'd turned his ship thirty minutes earlier.

Or even fifteen.

Or ten.

Because then the Foxhound would never have met the Isabel Anne. Or the heavy cruiser flying the Spanish Nationalist flag.

It was the lookout that spotted the smoke, almost on a reciprocal of their previous heading. And smoke it was, great oily clouds of it, whatever ship it was had decided to strain every ounce of speed out of her engines. She was obviously fleeing, flying along as if pursued by every legion that Hell possessed.

He had swung the Foxhound around, glad of the excitement, happy to order the ship to run at full speed, boredom forgotten in the excitement. Swiftly the Foxhound closed the distance, her turbines humming happily, glad to stretch their legs.

A ship was revealed, a worn and stained tramp steamer and at her stern, half hidden by the billowing smoke was a ragged and torn red ensign.

And that made the difference.

Later he explained over and over again to sympathetic admirals and less understanding politicians that the stained flag made what he did later inevitable.

Had to make a difference.

They were in international waters, only just, but still in open water. So he began to signal the steamer which anxiously altered course to meet him. It was then that they saw the second ship, the ship that the steamer was determined to avoid.

At first, he thought it was a friend, one of the County class heavy cruisers which an overburdened Navy occasionally sent through to add a little muscle to the destroyer screen, but there were subtle differences that caused him to doubt just a little.

Then all doubt was removed as the cruiser fired her forward eight-inch guns.

It was long range and the ship was firing almost directly into the risen sun, but it was obvious that the ship was determined to stop the steamer and four, two hundred- and fifty-six-pound projectiles were a powerful sign of her displeasure and her intent.

He remembered no hesitation as he gave the orders. He was calm and deliberate; his crew would detect no sense of alarm in his voice as they ran to action stations.

His radio operator began to urgently call the cruiser, asking her to cease fire and to identify herself, pointing out that all three ships were in international waters.

The cruiser was more than hull up on the horizon now, her bow wave brightly visible.

The Foxhound had nearly reached the steamer and was beginning to gracefully curve around the steamer, seeking to place herself between the cruiser and the rust stained vessel when the second salvo was fired.

It was an accident he later realised, in fact a whole series of accidents and assumptions. But that didn't help his conscience, didn't help when the memories stuck to the inside of his eyelids and stayed there night after sleepless night. Because one, just one shell of that salvo hit his ship.

The Foxhound like all her class was designed to be an all-purpose policeman, as comfortable in the Atlantic as in the muddy waters of the Yangtze. If the flag needed showing then the Foxhound, replete with guns, torpedoes and depth charges was more than willing to comply. Within her limitations she was a well-designed ship.

What she was never designed to do was withstand an eight-inch shell, no matter how poorly aimed, or how unintended.

The shell fired at long range plunged down on 'X' turret, which instantly vanished along with all its supporting structure. A gaping hot hell now appeared in Foxhound and she lurched and staggered under the impact. Flames instantly began to roar, loader and more fiercely every second.

There was no answer from the engine room and for a very long time no power, but Osbourne, wakened from his torpor, had brought up an emergency pump and was very sensibly directing the single jet of water not on the inferno that was formerly X turret, but on the depth charge and torpedoes that lay beyond. How much water got through the flames was debatable, but just one of those devices contained enough Explosive to complete the job so well begun by the cruiser.

He could not remember being afraid, he would have liked to have taken comfort from that, but he knew that he was too busy to be afraid. Everyone was busy that day, everyone apart from the ones that were still and quiet and would never be busy again. He was too busy to notice when the cruiser came surging up, boarding the Isabel Anne which lay dejected and supine, shocked into submission.

Within a very few moments both ships began to move off, the cruiser apologising for not rendering assistance pointing out that to do so would make her a target for potential enemies.

At that point he didn't care, although he knew that his ship would still float he had a host of other problems that were far more important than departing Spanish cruisers. But his problems were only just beginning because a half-ruined ship left him no choice.

No choice at all.


Mamma had taken her to the docks to see the English ship. Naturally she had taken her friend the doll, who though she still had the same fixed smile as ever, was now sporting a new haircut courtesy of an incident with Mamma's best pair of scissors.

At the time she thought the new style was a good idea, but now after a few days she was beginning to change her mind. After much reflection she thought that perhaps a haircut that left her friend bald on one side of her head was not such a good idea after all. Still there she was at the docks staring at the ugly ship, one hand clutching her friend, the other held firmly in her mother's grasp.

And it was an ugly ship, parts of it were painted grey but the back of it was very dirty and black and it had holes in it as well. She wasn't very impressed, the fishing boats that Papa had taken her to see were much nicer, though they smelled horribly of fish.

Mamma explained that the English ship had been attacked and had come here because the sailors on it were injured and had to go to hospital.

She looked up at the top of the ship and saw a tired looking man wearing a cap with a badge on it. She thought he looked very sad.

Suddenly he smiled and winked at her. It was a very slow wink with just a hint of comedy in it.

She jumped a little and then smiled and waved.

The man smiled again and then the ugly ship began to leave.

The people around her were silent, but she noticed that some of them were crying.


The eleven dead had been buried at sea.

He'd read the service himself, forcing himself to speak the words carefully and calmly, trying to make his voice louder than the wind and the waves.

The bodies, weighted down were tilted into the water and vanished with barely a splash, waiting as the service said until the day when the sea shall give up its dead. He wondered what he would say to those men on that fateful day. Would he say that they died because he was bored and was looking for a chance for excitement, a diversion to break the monotony? Or would he say it was his duty and theirs also to investigate any incident, no matter how trivial? Perhaps he would tell them that it was a mistake, that the Spanish cruiser never meant to kill them at all. Perhaps the dead didn't care, and it was only the living that fretted over causes and reasons.

Either way he still had a badly damaged ship and more than thirty wounded. Worse than that he had no doctor on board and limited medical supplies. The decision he then took was both easy and one he believed would end his career.

Spain was less than a day's steaming away even at the reduced speed which was all the engineers could coax out of his damaged ship. Less than a day's steaming away were doctors, clean bandages and morphine.

He hoped.

He could have waited for help, he could have tried for a French port, but the sight of those bandaged bodies and the look of helpless despair in the eyes of his sick berth attendant made up his mind.

Forty-eight hours to take on medical supplies and find doctors. Forty- eight hours to patch a ship. That would be enough, and surely no one could complain.

It was too late now in any event. He looked down onto the dockyard where a large crowd had gathered. Somehow the rumour had started that the blasted and smoke-stained Foxhound was the vanguard of a mighty British fleet which was even now just over the horizon. In a few moments the crowd was going to be bitterly disappointed.

He looked down at the dockside and his eyes locked on two figures. The first was a woman in her early thirties, close by her was a small child with a rather disreputable looking doll clutched in her hand. Both were looking up at him and their hopeful stares forced from him a smile for the woman and a wink for the little girl.

He gave the orders and the Foxhound left; slowly at first, but then with gathering speed until the woman, the girl and the doll were left far behind, lost in the destroyer's wake.

It wasn't much of a gift he left behind, a smile and a wink, but it was all he was allowed to give.

He never knew he gave a far greater gift to others.


Jorge tried to control the shivering, but his body overrode his mind and continued to desperately conserve heat. Spending the early winter in the Sierra de Cueras was not a game for children, but the mountains were theirs.

Theirs.

Bought with blood, with screams and terrible loss.

Here all around him covered in a white shroud of snow were the shallow graves of his friends; buried while the shells still fell. This is where they had stopped them, this is where cunning, and guile had for the moment defeated force. And best of all it was the forces of General Franco who had placed the weapon in their hand.

If the British ship had not been forced to seek shelter in Gijón then they would never have been able to spread the rumour that the Royal Navy had decided to add its weight to the Republican cause.

It was all too easy. A deliberately careless word spoken in the dockyard had spread like an oil stain. A prisoner interrogated by a 'British' officer had been allowed to escape. And that was all it took to sow fast growing seeds of doubt in the minds of the Nationalists; their attack faltered, stuttered and finally died, leaving the gateway to Northern Spain still in Republican hands.

For now.

Until the spring thaw revealed the graves and The Nationalists massed again.

A tight smile appeared on his wind cracked face as he wondered just what his famous ancestor would think of him crouched in the snow like a frightened rabbit. According to family legend over a hundred years ago his ancestor had been a famous general, mounted on a magnificent white charger, the commander of thousands and best of all the possessor of a magic gun that could fire huge cannon balls with unerring accuracy. He had sat on his grandmother's knee times without number and listened to the tales. As a child he had been entranced, a true believer, today as a man approaching his twenty second birthday he was not so sure.

His family were peasants, with the occasional blacksmith or artisan thrown in. That and no more. There were no aristocrats in his family tree, of that he was certain. At best his ancestor was a ragged guerrilla with a stolen mule.

He wondered what his own descendants would think of him. Would they tell of a bored man who had left his brothers farm to fight and found that he had a skill for it? Would they speak of a man who swiftly became a master of reconnaissance and ambush? That a rifle felt more natural in his hands than the shepherds crook? That he had risen through the ranks and would, if he lived rise still further?

He did not know and of course would never know.

He shivered again and stirred a little, bringing to his eyes his favourite possession. The binoculars were magnificent and a parting gift from an Italian who was unwise enough to come within range of Jorge's rifle.

He scanned the far ridge which was his to guard.

Nothing.

Scan again.

Nothin...There!

The merest flurry of sliding snow.

It might be a foolish goat desperate for forage, but even the most foolish of goats would realise that there would be nothing edible under the snow.

Only man would be foolish enough to cross the snow.

Scan. Eyes tight against the glare. More tracks in the snow. Count them. One through sixty; a small patrol seeking gaps in their lines.

He signalled to his men, who gave him snow crusted smiles in return.

This would be easy. Long ago he had mapped in his mind every bush and every rock in the valley. The ambush would be as he planned, all but a fortunate handful of the enemy would die, the rest bleeding and wounded would return to spread alarm and despondency.

He didn't have the white charger of his ancestor, nor did he command an army and an old rifle was enough magic in his hands.

And that would have to do.


Churchill deliberately put a large amount of scornful disbelief in his voice, he was tired of how the conversation was going, and had decided to force the issue. 'Is the Prime Minister suggesting that the young man in question acted incorrectly or illegally because if that is the position he wishes to take...'

Chamberlain's thin, reedy voice over rode the growl. 'You are deliberately misinterpreting my words. All I am saying is that the actions of the Foxhound have placed this government in a most unfortunate position. His arrival at the Republican held port of Gijón, however briefly, caused the Nationalist forces to break off their attack on that area believing that we had decided to intervene on behalf of the defenders. Other nations have asked whether this government has had a change of policy regarding Spain and that if it has then...'

Churchill knew that he had no supporters around the table and that he was fighting a lone and losing battle, which of course made it all the more imperative that he should make his point. 'May I remind the Prime Minister and this cabinet that the Foxhound had been damaged in an unprovoked attack and that...'

Lord Halifax broke in. 'It was an accident. The Nationalists apologised!'

Churchill turned his gaze on the Foreign Minister. 'And how pray tell do we accept an apology from an organisation which is in open rebellion to its own legally appointed government, an organisation, which by the way Minister, His Majesty's Government does not recognise as a legal combative?

Halifax fell silent and Churchill continued.

'As I was saying, after being damaged the captain of the Foxhound elected to proceed to the nearest friendly port in order to make repairs and to enlist medical aid for his wounded.'

He allowed a little heavy irony to enter his voice. 'It may come as somewhat of a surprise to some of you gentlemen, but his Majesty's destroyers are not over equipped with medical personnel or supplies, and as the Foxhound had thirty-one wounded men and was far from any other friendly ships the captain took the only sensible and humane course of action.

That is an action with which I am in full accord. It may be that his it has caused this government some embarrassment, but if we are honest with ourselves that is in part the fault of our policy towards Spain. Both sides contending for power in that unhappy country have perhaps more of the devil than the divine in their make-up and we have decided only to be resolute only in our distaste for either side, but one of his Majesty's ships has been attacked, men wearing the Kings uniform were killed and injured. And we have stood idly by, and that is a terrible thing to see. If we wish to see a repeat of this we only have to do nothing, if our flag, our vaunted power is to become a hollow mockery we need do nothing but sit on our hands. If we wish our voice in the councils of mankind to dwindle and be counted not amongst the powerful we need but accept this outrage.

'That is the choice that we must make now. If we rise to this challenge then an ounce of courage, of direction and spirit now may save much effort and many tears in the future.

Halifax broke in. 'And just what do you suggest First Lord; a cutting out expedition against the Spanish? This isn't the eighteenth century you know, and a more active role by us risks a general war, another Great War. The country would not stand for such a policy, we'd be turned out of office in an instant.

'Are you willing to risk that over a single incident, an incident which we have no proof was a deliberate act and may well, as the Nationalists claim, have happened within Spanish territorial waters.'

Churchill's defeat was beginning. He knew that Halifax had the backing of the Prime Minister and the cabinet and this meeting was as much about party politics as foreign policy, but he had to try, and in trying salvage some gains. 'Are you suggesting, Foreign Secretary, that the word of a Spanish rebel is to be taken over the sworn testimony of a Royal Navy officer?'

Halifax shrugged. 'Mistakes happen, charts can be in error. Even your captain agreed that the Foxhound was only just outside the limit. We cannot risk war, a war for which we are not ready or afford over a matter of interpretation of a line on a chart. Surely you can see that?'

It was an appeal for reason that had been echoed by many of the press Barons, and Churchill knew that to push too hard against public opinion would risk the gains he had already made. The cabinet was wrong, and he knew it, defiance in defeat was a fine principle, but it did not apply in every case and certainly did not apply here.

Now was a time for cunning so he put on the rueful smile of the defeated and hoped for the best. 'As you say Foreign Secretary, but in that case the new rules for captains of His Majesty's ships around Spanish waters should now apply? Purely as a temporary measure', he added in seeming haste.

Halifax looked around the room and received approving nods. 'I'm sure that I can see no reason why not...purely as a temporary measure of course. Prime Minister?'

Chamberlain nodded. 'Yes I agree, none of us wish to see a repetition of that deplorable incident and if such rules make it less likely then so be it'.

Churchill had been watching the Prime Minister with puzzlement for the past hour. While not actually moving the man gave the impression of squirming in his seat with suppressed excitement.

He soon found out why.

The French Prime Minister had called for a meeting to discuss the whole question of the Spanish civil war, but before that Lord Halifax would be visiting Berlin.

He had been out manoeuvred.

# PAVED WITH GOOD INTENTIONS

The music broke over him in waves, each wave more powerful and more compelling than before. They transported him to a world where Gods and mortals contended for power, where magic was all around, and emotion was a living pulse. For the moment he was not the Fuhrer, not a politician, still less the man of destiny that he believed himself to be. No, tonight he was just a man acknowledging Wagner's genius and the undoubted skill of the Nuremberg Opera company.

The cares of the outside world were blocked out and he was alone with Wagner's music. Tonight he could relax and follow destiny's path with all the assurance of a sleepwalker.

Tonight marked a new beginning for Germany.

Tonight he would make good another of his promises and join his homeland with the Reich.

It was a gamble, but the odds were in his favour. France was split with sectarian riots, England still under the illusion he could be managed, Poland too aware of the bear on her borders. Czechoslovakia terrified and Italy now bound by the blood oath of her leader to march with him. Spain, where blood flowed.

No one would interfere. Oh there would be polite notes which would be as politely received, and politely ignored.

Of that he was certain.

While the worlds gaze was distracted he would strike.

He looked down as the play began.

On stage a tall woman sings of love and betrayal. In Austria a border is dissolved.

A hero appears searching for magic, and in Vienna the arrests begin.

The orchestra utters awful warnings and an army marches south.

The hero is reunited with his one true love.

And Austria is no more.

From overture to finale, from first scene to last chorus. In that time, in that small instant a coup is born, takes its first breath, screams lustily and takes control. The final chords fade so slowly that no man could truly say when the last note sounded.

For a moment he sat entranced only for the spell to be broken as an aide whispered in his ear. While he sat a nation had died. He could now face the world with an innocent face, the world would of course grumble and then forget.

Until the next time.


No one was more surprised than Leon Blum was when his words had caused his government to collapse.

It wasn't a very good government even by French standards, and it certainly wasn't a strong one, but all the same to see it throw up its hands and die before his eyes was astonishing. The resulting wave of elections had washed him into the office of Prime Minister and there he had stayed, his talents given free rein, and as always at the service of France.

But not all of France.

The hatred and contempt shown to him by the right was matched by the scorn and mistrust hurled at him by the left. To the left he was not pure enough, and to the right any tinge of red was a shade too much. He had enemies of course, as the nation's chief political surgeon he had sometimes wielded the scalpel and on more than one occasion the bludgeon. Twice now his views had put him in danger and he still bore the scars from the last attempt. A foolish attempt which had only strengthened his will.

But will power alone was not enough, his government, made up of so many strands of opinion was becoming impossible to hold together and soon he must resign, and his cabinet must follow.

Too many in his government wanted France to take an active role in the turmoil to the south. It was an attractive proposition he had to admit. To fight the enemies of his conscience in another country had a certain appeal.

But if she did, then France would fight alone. The British had made that clear some time ago and the best that he could gain was a meaningless neutrality which effectively starved the Republicans while allowing the rebels to gorge on men and supplies blatantly brought to their door. And if she fought, then the sickness which infected Spain would jump the Pyrenees and his country would descend into chaos. With no guarantee that Republican Spain would survive even then.

France had a trembling grip on stability and sanity and that above all could not be sacrificed. His government, a coalition united only by mutual hate had begun to eat itself and could no longer lay claim to legitimacy. Better to leave now, before the bloodletting became too extreme. But better to leave on his terms, turns which left room for a return.

To resign now would be to draw accusations of cowardice down on his head. The Right would say that they had frightened him into resigning, the Left that they had expelled a traitor. This would only encourage more acts of violence and more death, as well as ruining his political career. No, that avenue was unthinkable.

Yet there was a road that could save him.

The international situation could, if he was careful buy France time to deal with her domestic problems. The solution was very simple and at the same time highly impractical. He would call for a conference of the great powers to discuss the whole Spanish question. If there was no war then there could be a much-reduced French involvement in Spanish affairs, thereby removing a great source of friction within his country. Of course such a scheme would fail, but when it failed his government would fall and he with it. At one stroke his resignation would be for political reasons and not at the behest of either side of a divided France.

It was, he thought at first glance a plausible idea.

The communists could hardly argue against a peace conference, especially if the U.S.S.R was invited. Of course there would be no positive outcome and possibly no meeting at all.

So what possible harm could it do?


'It's all a bloody mess'.

Bevan winced at the profanity and hid his distaste by taking a long sip of the hotel's excellent tea. He looked out of the window, Blackpool seafront even in summer was not a place for the weak and feeble, and now in the depths of winter only the truly brave or the truly foolhardy confronted weather generated by a malicious Irish sea. Despite that a few couples still walked along the sea wall, eyes half shut against icy winds and blown sand. 'Sooner them, than me', he thought and turned his attention back to the table.

'We know its bloody mess Herbert; the question is how are we going to respond?' Wilkinson's question was asked mildly; as a member of Attlee's shadow cabinet she outranked Herbert Morrison, but she never forgot that he ruled London almost as a private fiefdom. He was in fact the nearest thing to an American political boss that she'd ever seen.

She'd formed an uneasy alliance with Bevan which would never, ever blossom into friendship. Both were determined though that Labour Party policy must change direction, the old shibboleths which ruled them no longer served.

Morrison, much as she suspected refused to be diverted. 'What can we do Ellen? You of all people should know just what a mess Spain is in. It's all very well people saying that we must take a more active stance, that we must aid the Spanish who are fighting Fascism, but which group do we aid? The Socialists, the Moscow Communists, the anti-Moscow communists, the Trotskyists or perhaps the Anarchists, who I needn't remind you are looked upon as little better than Fascists by what passes for Republican government these days.

'I'm all for fighting Fascism, but Spain is not a place where we can make a difference, and we need to very careful. Look what happened to Blum, his own Popular Front party tears him from office and then splinters into factions again. The Russians and the Italians damn near come to blows…at a peace conference Ellen of all places! Our own government deliberately did everything it could to frustrate Blum's attempts at mediation, and if that wasn't bad enough our Prime Minister tries to do a behind the scenes deal with Hitler, who not only declines the offer, but declines it very publicly.

'We could split the Party over this Ellen, very, very easily and then where would we be? Certainly not in a position to win in 1940. We should be looking inwards, not outwards that's where the votes lie Ellen…in Manchester not Madrid!' He looked around, beaming at his clever use of words hoping for support but not seeing any.

Wilkinson remembered Attlee's comment *We need London, so we need Morrison, it's that simple, but he doesn't see much beyond Tower Hill, so let him ramble and then let Dalton loose, when the time is right you know what to do.'* She wondered just what arguments his friend had used on his rival, but as Morrison looked around the room and sought allies he knew that the man was about to be bitterly surprised. Maybe Attlee didn't need much, Dalton saw much further than Morrison.

'No'.

The voice was not loud, nor was it soft, but it did, as Attlee had predicted come from Dalton, the one man that Morrison believed would be his strong right arm. Dalton ignored the flash of anger that crossed his friend's face and continued. 'Ellen asked how are we to respond, not whether? It's a fair question and it deserves answering.

'A year ago, six months even we wouldn't be having this conversation, wouldn't need to for that matter; the country didn't care about Spain and neither did we. But a lot has changed recently. That navy ship got shelled and that stirred things up a bit, and now Hitler marches into Austria at the request of provisional government made up of Nazi sympathisers. People are beginning to notice and ask questions and if...' he nodded to Morrison. 'If we want to be elected in 1940 we'd better have answers.

'So where do we fight? Where can we make a difference, more importantly where can we be seen to be different?'

He paused, and Wilkinson took her chance. 'Where, or should that be how?'

Bevan smiled inwardly, this was his chance. He took the paper from his folder and threw it theatrically onto the table. 'This is how, it's just a draft, but this is how we make a difference, here and abroad'.

And then the arguments broke out anew.


There had been debate and anger. Hard words and insults had been spoken. Threats had been issued, not subtle threats but declarations of intent, fuelled by passion. But they were not masters in their own house. Grim reality stood ever watchful, ever menacing over them.

A conference designed for peace had died before it could take more than a few breaths.

Franco held the lands that lay to the South

For the moment they were safe shielded by mountains and winter ice.

This was a brief respite. For the people of Northern Spain were cut off, isolated and alone. Now there was only one path to take. The arguments died away, slowly for passions ran deep, but when the silence was complete the words were read.

"We the people of Asturias do solemnly declare that we are a free and sovereign nation, with all the rights and duties that do obtain to that state...'

The words ran on for what seemed to many to be an eternity, but at the end they were committed.

There would be, there could be no turning back. Asturias would be free.

Or die.

# HALFWAY BACK

It had cost him an entire crate of India pale ale as a bribe and even then, the records clerk had grumbled. 'If he's such a good friend of yours, then how is it that you don't have his address?'

Pulver had made no answer but gently pushed the wooden crate behind the man's desk. No other words had been spoken but a crumpled piece of paper had been placed in his hand. Now he had the address of the man who had sent him on his journey, the man who had begun to teach him the love of practical mathematics and applied force that was engineering. The man who had vanished. They shook hands that day on the deck of the empty Hood and that was the last he'd seen of the old engineer. The Navy had swallowed him up, and Pulver was certain that he'd never see him again.

And now the man was his only hope.

So he began to write.

There were several draughts of the letter, each one savagely crumpled into a tight ball of paper and thrown viciously towards, but never quite into the waste basket. How to ask a man so reticent, so far above him for help? And the man had already favoured him far more than Pulver believed he deserved. To ask for help again smacked of rudeness or worse. And yet he must somehow serve again on the Hood.

At least he thought he could ask for advice, for despite his desire, he could not bring himself to ask for help. And so the letter was posted to an almost unpronounceable address in Scotland. As Pulver posted the letter he imagined it speeding on its way, carried by a powerful engine spurting hot steam as it travelled far to the North.

And he waited for a reply.

And waited.

A week went by, then two. He began to despair; his approach had been justifiably rebuffed.

It was towards the end of the third week when the postcard bearing a second-class stamp arrived.

In a plain, workmanlike hand it gave a telephone number, a date and instructions to ring promptly at a certain time. The word *promptly* was underlined thickly in purple ink and he smiled a little at the thought that the grim old engineer's habits had not changed.

It was exactly the right time when the operator connected him with the far away number. He heard the phone ring and then a lilting voice answering. 'The Clachaig Inn, who is it that is speaking?'

And then a long familiar voice heard in the background. 'That would be for me.'

For a moment the voice transported Pulver back to that fateful day in the Hood's engine room and a man with a grip of steel threatening him with horrible punishments. He wondered if it was not too late to put the phone down and write the whole idea off as a bad idea. And then it was indeed too late.

'Pulver?'

Pulver squeaked an affirmative and there was a dry almost mocking laugh.

'Yes that sounds like you, I got your letter. My God man you're not asking much. You got lucky once and now you want a second chance?' The phone crackled as the engineer's voice rose a few decibels. 'When the Hood comes out of dry dock they'll be admiral's sons queueing outside the dockyard gates for a place on her. There is not a chance of you being asked back on her.'

Pulver's heart sank and his fingers began to relax on the phone, but the voice continued. 'Unless...'

Pulver's pulse stopped and then started again, but another train of thought had begun in the old engineer's mind. 'Mr Pulver, I know you had a good eye, nothing much escaped you. Do you still have that, or has promotion removed that gift?'

Pulver managed to convince the man that a single, thin gold line on his sleeve had not changed him.

The answer seemed to please the old engineer. 'Good, Pulver, do you know how long I was in the Navy before they beached me?' Pulver was about to reply when the man wistfully answered his own question. 'Thirty-six years Pulver, thirty-six years. I joined the year the old queen died. I've seen a few things in that time and watched more than one man rise, aye and helped them on their way.'

The wistful tone left, and his voice grew serious. 'I've called in a favour for you boy. It's the last favour I can do for you. An old friend of mine runs the Navy inspection office at Jarrow. He'll put in a request for you, bearing in mind you have previous experience on the Hood. Maybe you'll do no more than fetch and carry but you'll have advantage of knowing how she's been rebuilt and that will give you a head start over all those admiral's sons.'

Pulver began to stammer out his thanks but the old man brusquely interrupted. 'Nonsense boy. Nonsense. The good of the service, that's all that needs to be considered.' The voice dropped a little as if he wished the conversation to be more private. 'You heard her didn't you, that last day before we paid off?'

Pulver had been there that day amidst the temporary repairs which had enabled the Hood to sail home. Each girder, each plate had groaned and screamed, the sounds melding into a single song of complaint and pain. If he was mad for believing in such things then so was the old engineer, so what harm could be done if he admitted it? 'Yes I heard her, that's why I want to go back sir.'

Pulver heard a soft chuckle. 'That's what I thought, she got to you as well. She's a grand old lady, and from what I've heard she'll be better yet before too long. Look after her for me won't you Pulver?'

Pulver promised that he would and again tried to stammer out his thanks.

The last words he heard from the old engineer was a soft 'For the good of the service'. Then there was a harsh click and Pulver was left holding a silent telephone. He placed the telephone gently back on its cradle, not willing to believe his luck and half believing that it would ring again with the old engineer explaining it had all been a terrible mistake or worse a very bad joke. He stood fixed in space for several seconds, daring the telephone to ring, but it never did, and he began to walk away with many a backwards glance at the red painted box. It took him nearly an hour to recognise the feeling that had begun to glow within him.

It was the feeling of coming home.


Were they blue or were they grey?

He couldn't make up his mind about the eyes, but the face was undoubtedly pretty. The face looked up at him and her questioning smile made Pulver blush and he began to stammer out his introduction.

It had been a long weekend. The great steam engine had thrust him and two hundred of his fellow passengers through the night north to Crew where the temporary friendships forged out comfortable silence were permanently sundered, never to rise again. From there he crossed the vast floodlit railway concourse to where a small, neglected looking engine was coupled to carriages which undoubtedly had seen better days though he doubted that any of those days would be recent ones. He refused though to allow the unkempt carriage to dampen his spirits; he was returning to the best place on earth and the second-class carriage with its faint odour of urine and disinfectant was not going to spoil the occasion.

So nodding politely to his fellow passengers he did what every true born Englishman did in the company of strangers and erected a barrier of newspaper and retreated behind it.

The news was almost uniformly bad.

Yet another interim government had arisen in France, this time under Pierre Laval who had promised elections in early spring. The last French Prime Minster had been seen taking the waters at Aix le Bain seemingly undaunted by either his loss of position or his expulsion from his own party. Japan and Russia were carrying out an undeclared war in the Far East with all the usual tales of human misery. Germany was digesting its last meal, and already there were tales of trials and arrests across Austria.

The newspaper seemed determined to conspire with the worn-out carriage to depress him, so he took refuge in sleep.

The following morning found him safely housed in a cheap boarding house and walking in his number one uniform with his orders carefully secured towards Jarrow's dockyard. He approached the door of the small shed which was all a parsimonious Navy would provide for its inspection team. He knocked and was greeted by the beautiful eyes in the pretty face.

Minutes later he was in another office meeting a naval officer who didn't have beautiful eyes or have a face which could be described in any way as pretty. Within the hour Pulver was equipped with a boiler suit, given plans and drawings and was walking towards where his ship was being reborn.

For the moment all thoughts of blue, or possibly grey eyes was driven from his mind.

But only for the moment.


David Riley put the telephone down with a sense of satisfaction and placed a victorious tick next to the name neatly typed on a worn sheet of paper.

Only fifty pounds pledged from that mayor, but that was understandable; his small town made only a tiny contribution to the Hood, just one firm and that employing less than a hundred men. But it was still fifty pounds and more importantly another voice.

It was the big cities that he had targeted and targeted successfully. Birmingham, Leeds, Manchester, industrial giants all, were strong enough to resist any pressure from the shipbuilder's cartel. They cared little for such things; they were business cities first last and always. Where they led others followed.

The idea of cities buying the Treasury bonds initially floated for the rebuilding of the Hood and using that link to form a special interest group had taken off.

And taken off far quicker than he had dared imagine.

There was now a serious challenge to the voice of the shipbuilder's federation who still championed the cause of limiting ship building to yards that they alone controlled.

Other voices had now been raised.

And though he was mayor of Jarrow, it looked like he was about to undertake new duties.

David Riley was now a choir master.


For Neville Chamberlain there simply was no alternative. He'd accepted the German takeover of Austria. The public, the newspapers had recognised that short of sanctions or even war there was little that could be done. He'd judged the mood well, there simply was no appetite to interfere in what many saw as a logical, even necessary event. The arrests, the violence which Austria suffered were ignored and soon forgotten.

The Nazi run plebiscite that followed had confirmed that his decision not to act had been correct. Germany and Austria were now one nation and he had averted a crisis.

He had begun to formulate plans to slowly increase his governments influence abroad.

It was then when Atlee struck.

The Labour party sponsored the Asturian government to appear before a committee of the League of Nations. It wasn't a very influential committee, but that wasn't the point, because the Asturian representatives handed over not only their own plebiscite but an emotional appeal for recognition as a sovereign nation.

And then the attacks began.

Atlee had long since recognised that in Ellen Wilkinson he had a publicist whose skills were unequalled and just as in the last election campaign he drew upon her strength.

A series of articles and interviews appeared. They weren't bright or colourful, but thoughtful and balanced. They sought no outright support, nor did they demand direct action but asked only for sympathy and understanding. It was a subtle campaign, cheap to run and unfortunately for the government remarkably effective.

Wilkinson had relied on the British public's well-known love for the underdog and played on that weakness with all the skill of a virtuoso violinist.

With the field well ploughed Atlee and the Labour Party struck. Their questions were deliberately and deceptively simple and were designed not only to trap his government but to put it on the wrong side of public opinion. The points were hammered home and hammered repeatedly. Why if the government had accepted the results of the Austrian plebiscite would it not accept any others? Why if Germany was allowed to promote the self determination of peoples was His Majesty's government doing everything in their power to frustrate the wishes of the Asturian people?

No answer and no counter attack by the government was able to do more than blunt the attack

A series of editorials supporting the government in the Times and the Daily Mail was answered by a savage cartoon by Zec in the Daily Mirror. It showed Chamberlain and Halifax resolutely turning their backs on an infant in a crib. Three other figures instantly recognisable as Hitler, Mussolini and Franco with knives drawn were creeping up on the small child. Zec, like all great cartoonists had condensed a complex situation into its essential elements.

The editorial which accompanied it was simply reinforcing what even the simplest reader could see. A small nation had arisen, reached out for help and been refused. As was often the case a picture was worth a thousand words and public support for the government began to slip. The cartoon was irritating in the extreme but was he had to admit extremely effective. The Labour party had found a stick and was using it without mercy.

With a by -election imminent he could not take the chance of a poor result or even a defeat and he had thought long on how to extract his government from the situation. His chosen solution would remove the stick from Labour's hand and possibly gave other advantages. He would put the proposal to cabinet tomorrow.

There would be little argument he was sure, Winston would complain of course but really there was simply no alternative. His armour was proof against both anger and satire. Harsh words and the scribblings of vitriolic journalists could no longer hurt him. He would recognise Asturias as a combatant, but at the same time give the same recognition to the forces of General Franco.

He would at one stroke be able to be able to claim neutrality with a policy of even handedness, while being able at the same time to suggest that now Germany and Italy could remove their forces from Spain and concentrate on a political solution. He smiled a little at the thought, perhaps this time some good may come out of the Spanish Debacle. What ever happened he was sure that this time he had wrenched the stick out of Labour's hand.


The plumb bob hung vertically down, pulled by the irresistible forces of gravity, while the bubble in the spirit level gave silent praise to his growing skill.

All in all it wasn't a bad wall.

And it had served its purpose.

It had brought a little bit of calm to the anger that filled him. Brick by brick his thoughts had begun to clear. It was odd that a man who in the ordinary course of events would not have had to stoop to physical labour had found solace in the laying of bricks and the trowelling of mortar. Odd but true.

He could see things now a little clearer now. He'd given warning long before Atlee had begun his campaign. Long before Asturias became a nation and long before Vienna ceased to be one. His voice was lost in the tumult and was lost still. And yet he was still at fault, his pride had been his undoing.

The voice had whispered to him like the Sirens of old. 'Now is the hour', it had said, 'Join them and convince them. Use your words, use your mastery and advance'.

He had succumbed and let vanity lead him. A place on the cabinet was his, bought by right he thought. But he could not convince them, and his vaunted mastery broke on the adamantine wall of Chamberlain's convictions.

Brick by brick that wall had been built and the wall muffled his voice and closed off his warnings.

Chamberlain controlled the cabinet, Churchill's allies, actual or potential were too weak to do more than look on. He had entered a prison, and there was only one key left. He cleaned his tools with what he hoped was professional care and as the long shadows of a dying day began to merge he walked into his study.

As the anger had left him the typewriter keys were persuaded to give substance to his thoughts, rather than hammered into submission. It took an hour to fashion his key, but at the end he knew it would work. With great care as befitted such an important document he signed his full name to his resignation from the cabinet.

He was free.

For now.


Gijon had long been a city, long been a port, and now it was a self-proclaimed capital. The Republic of Asturias had been proclaimed, the Basques to the east had risen from their mountains and asserted that they too were a free people. Tonight the wine ran freely, tonight the music played and the people smiled. They thought they had won, they thought that Chamberlain's declaration had freed them, broken every difficulty. This was victory. This was freedom.

It was neither.

The faces smiled in vain and the wine flowed from cups made of delusions. The road ahead was steep and narrow, the chances of success no better today than they were yesterday. If the coming battle could be won, then everything could change.

They could fight on.

A success, even a stalemate would give them that which they needed most of all.

Time.

Time to borrow money, time to buy arms. Time to encourage friends and convince the undecided. Time to draw breath and wait for better days.

Asturias must pray for better days.

After all what choice did she have?


It looked real.

There were trenches where trenches should be. Machine gun posts where even the most foolish of commanders would place them. There was even a dilapidated ambulance with a faded red cross prominently displayed. As a piece of theatre it could not be beaten. And everything about it was false.

The trenches only appeared to be deep. The machine guns were made of wood, while the ambulance was more canvas than Citroen.

This was the gate. This valley was the highway that the enemy must take. A winter that would not die gave Jorge time. Time that he had not wasted. By day his stage set grew but slowly, an easy prey to spying eyes and circling aircraft. But by night the energy saved was expended and more than expended. Trees were partially cut, mountain streams needed but moments to be dammed, cliffs were cunningly set with explosives.

And at the valley entrance lay the greatest surprise.

Asturias had few friends and even less resources, and small chance of gaining either in the near future. What it did have was Jorge and his ragged army. They didn't have white horses and there was a shocking lack of magic cannons, but though they lacked all those essential items they did have a fierce determination and a rough unlettered captain to lead them.

And that would have to do.


Fifteen feet.

The great frame hung from the crane.

Thirteen feet.

The wire ropes began to turn a little slower in the pulleys.

Ten feet.

The frame stopped, swaying gently in the rain-soaked wind.

Pulver could do nothing but watch. There were no drawings to check here, no inspections, no forms to be filled in. Here he was a bystander, a watcher on sufferance, bound to silence.

Stop.

The frame swaying in a sea born wind.

Patient, ever patient. Eyes long hardened to every difficulty checked and checked again in a time-honoured ritual as solemn as any church ceremony. Men's lives and more importantly their reputations were at stake here. A grease stained hand was waved, and the wires began to turn again.

Eight feet.

Then six.

The face far up in the crane house was only a white blob, but Pulver could feel the man's anxiety.

Four feet.

Then three.

Men began to appear, long used tools in their waiting hands. Pulver sensed rather than felt the rain coursing down.

Three feet.

Then two.

The wires creaked, and the pulleys turned slower than any hour hand.

Twelve inches.

Then six.

The frame began to slide into the keel now. Pulver's heart jumped with every screech and jar.

Two inches.

Hydraulic rams strained to achieve what simple gravity could not.

One inch.

Nothing.

Stop.

Pulver stopped breathing but could detect no panic in the men. Long heavy hammers fell in unison. And the frame settled with crash that shook his boots. It was over. The great stern frame was in.

And the race to finish the Hood had begun.


The reverberation flowed down her like a river.

No part of her was immune to the sound. New parts and old. Large or small. All felt the sound.

The sound pleased her, for she knew it for what is was. The last difficulty had been erased, her friends had won the last battle. Her patience had its reward. Soon now she would be complete and a warrior once more. Soon she could face the world.

She was the Hood and a new life lay before her.


The man was so infuriating!

His reports were works of art, without so much as a comma out of place. No detail however obscure was omitted. He was unfailingly polite to all he met and had never been known to utter a harsh word. His superiors had nothing but praise for him. In her eyes he was almost perfect except for one infuriating sin.

He would not talk to her.

Oh they had whole conversations, sometimes as much as three stammering sentences, but even then his eyes, which were she admitted very pretty, could not stay focused on her. Instead he seemed to find great interest in the wall behind her head. He was undoubtedly the one, but how to catch him had eluded her.

Until now.

She intended to use his weakness against him.

The great grey huntress that lay behind her office would help her she was sure. She would ask Lieutenant Pulver for a guided tour of his ship.

He could not refuse.

And then she would make her move.


He did not stammer.

That was the first thing she noted. Once on board the diffident young man was transformed into the confident young officer. He walked throughout the Hood with her at his side and as he did so facts, figures and anecdotes fell from him.

He took her to the great gun turrets and showed her just how the massive shells would be brought up from the depths of the ship and on the bridge, she sat in the captain's chair and looked out as men carefully laid wooden planks in serried rows over armoured steel.

But it was in the engine rooms that the true man appeared and from that moment she knew she would always have a rival. The Hood and the slim man with the thin lieutenant's ring on his sleeve were linked in some undefinable way.

The evidence was plain enough. His hands were never still, always seeking to touch a white-faced dial or length of dully shining steel. And he spoke of the ship as if she was a living, breathing thing that could feel pain and love.

She was about to make a humorous rejoinder to this obviously absurd theory when she looked into his eyes and saw that he was absolutely serious. The words, half formed stumbled in her mouth, and when they rose they had transformed themselves into polite agreement.

This was the key to the man she decided, and also if she chose him her cross, for she would never fully own him.

The grey green eyes closed for a moment and then opened in decision. It was enough.

She moved in for the kill and began a dance ten thousand years old and yet brand new.

Pulver never knew that he had been hunted and caught, never knew that from the moment he entered the ship his life and hers would change.

And neither he nor his hunter heard the soft chuckle that came from the Hood.


The screams of adulation still rang loudly down the corridor as he strode away. The podium was empty now though the lights still shone above it. Yet still the cries continued as if by sheer force of sound and will they could bring their beloved Fuhrer back.

But tonight, for him the moment had passed. He'd had his fill of them, drunk deeply of their emotions, emotions that he had stirred. He'd felt every one of them, the anger, and the envy, the hate and the longing. He knew that the crowd's borrowed power would fade from him drop by drop until he was forced to return as the addict returns to the needle. But that day was far off. For now he had made his intentions plain.

The bastard child of Versailles must be bent to the will of the German people, they had defied that will for long enough. He had no more tolerance. The crowd had bayed their approval as he told them that the Germans in Czechoslovakia were not defenceless, nor had they been deserted. There must be justice for them.

His heart rate and his breathing slowed as the chants began to diminish and his mind began to range far away from Berlin. Chamberlain's move was an opportunity that he had not looked for yet he would be a fool not to take advantage of it. And to do so he would need to see two people very urgently. The first would be Goring, but the second and most important would be the French ambassador. It seemed as if the Spanish game had sparked back into life and he had just been dealt a new hand.


It had been a polite, almost jovial dismissal, but it was still a dismissal and as the great bronze doors closed behind him and he began the walk down the long marble floored corridor André François-Poncet began to tremble. He could not decide if the trembling was due to anger or fear, but as a diplomat he had not shown any emotion as the Fuhrer had explained the European situation as he saw it.

The British, he had explained had forced him to re-evaluate the German position regarding Spain. Oh he understood that Chamberlain's decision was due as much to British domestic politics as anything else, but it had put him in a terrible position.

Hitler, whatever else he might be, was a great actor and a less experienced man may very well have been deceived by the display of regret and dismay as it was explained to him that Germany, as the great champion of people's right to self-determination had been placed in a terrible position.

Naturally Germany could not discriminate between peoples.

'Even Bolsheviks', Hitler had told him gravely. Perhaps the British had not consulted with Paris? In any event he was giving serious consideration to following the British lead and as a sign of good faith had given orders that the German Condor Legion in Spain suspend its operations. 'The German people desire nothing more than a just peace, for themselves and for others.'

Naturally Poncet began to look for the true motives behind the statement. They weren't too had to find.

This was an attack on France.

The Spanish civil war which France had fought ferociously to contain and hoped to see end, would continue, and persist in being a rallying point for the left wing, worse than that it would always be a distraction and a threat to whatever Government sat in Paris.

It was Hitler who pointed out another disadvantage. Still keeping the grave demeanour which it seemed he thought appropriate for today's interview, he casually mentioned that if the Asturian Republic managed to achieve some sort of stability then that could only encourage the Basque nationalists who were fighting their own mountain campaign and were receiving semi covert support from their fellow Basques north of the Spanish border.

'It would be a pity if despite all our efforts the Spanish war was to spill over the border, but who should know better than Germany that the ties of blood and language will overcome any obstacles...even mountain ranges. The German people are naturally sympathetic to such urges.'

The words were spoken softly, not with the usual harsh voice and even the translator looked slightly uncertain at this change of pace. This was a naked threat against the political integrity of France; Hitler was using a new nation, whose creed he despised as a sword to hold over France.

'And', thought Poncet grimly, 'the temporary removal of the Condor Legion from Northern Spain was a reminder to General Franco that German largesse was not infinite in scope'. No doubt the growing confidence of the general had taken a severe knock, and Hitler had shown just where true power in Spain was exercised. A Republican presence, even a weak one in Northern Spain would keep both Paris and Madrid weaker and with fewer options.

He began to gently remind the Fuhrer that today's meeting was not about fledgling republics, but about French concern over the continued German pressure on Czechoslovakia. He ran through his prepared speech, and Hitler appeared to listen attentively, the grave, slightly enigmatic smile never leaving his face, but at the back of Poncet's mind was the threat that had been made earlier.

He finished speaking and was waiting for a reply, when in what was no doubt a pre-arranged move a smartly dressed aide came up and whispered in the Fuhrer's ear. Apologies were made, a matter of grave importance had come up and the meeting, enjoyable as it had been must be cut short. Perhaps Monsieur Poncet could consult with the German Foreign Office? He was sure that a solution could be found.

Of course it would have to be a solution that was acceptable to the German people, but he had great confidence in the French government's ability to recognise the plight of the Sudeten Germans and the justness of their cause. In the meantime it was regrettable...but.

As Poncet got into his car and was drive down through the flag encrusted streets he realised that there had come a time of sacrifice.

And it was his job to ensure those sacrifices were not made by France.

Where the hell were they?

Jorge scanned the sky, an open hand shielding his eyes in an instinctive action. His head moved across the sky, but there was nothing. A few lone aircraft buzzed across the valley, but where were the Germans? Every fibre of his body, every past experience had taught him to expect row after serried row of German aircraft to rain death and confusion on him. This was the way of war in Spain, death would fall from the skies long before the artillery, long before the infantry. But today the black painted aircraft were missing from the skies. The battle was beginning without them, and Jorge instantly began adapting his campaign. If the enemy had made a mistake he would take full advantage of it.

He paused for just a moment, the possibilities running through his head like fleeing deer. What if it was a trap, what if he was to commit his men and then find his skies once more owned by the enemy? He shivered despite the thick sheepskin he wore and decided not to chase phantom armies powered by imagination. As he began to give his orders the first enemy shells began to fall.

It was, as he expected an intense bombardment. The Fascists had spent time and effort to bring up heavy weapons expecting that these would win the battle and reduce their casualties. He watched as the shells erupted, each one an explosion of soil and rock.

The mock ambulance, the false machine posts all died, and died not once but many times. The trenches fell under a hard rain of death that poured on them without respite, without mercy. Nothing could have survived in those trenches and had they been filled with men he would have already suffered a grievous loss. It was a very great shame he thought with a grin that his men were placed anywhere but the trenches.

Through the morning gloom he saw the enemy advance.

They were confident. He could see that in the way they walked, they were sure that his thin, poorly equipped army had been decimated beyond any capacity to resist. Soon he would prove them wrong.

Victory, as his ancestor had proved was not always on the side of the big battalions but sometimes favoured those who used what they had as best they could. And Jorge had spent months using his natural talents for surprise and ambush to prepare for this battle.

He was ready, but more importantly the enemy was not.

He waited.

And waited.

He felt his lieutenants tense, willing him to give the order.

He waited.

Waited until every enemy soldier was where he needed them to be.

Waited until he was certain. And gave a single nod.

The earth heaved itself skywards in a massive fountains that carried men into the air and dropped their shattered bodies onto the insulted ground.

The winter had not been wasted; the valley had been honeycombed with tunnels and galleries, each and every one of them filled with kilo after kilo of explosives. He had closed the gate to the valley and trapped the enemy.

They would have no respite.

More orders and more explosions swiftly followed. Craters appeared in the valley, smaller this time and seemingly far less harmful, killing only a handful of men.

He smiled a bitter smile, feeling the enemy commander's confusion. 'Just wait my friend', he thought, 'and all will be revealed'.

At his command a dozen mountain streams, partially dammed these past months were released. The streams long denied true release and anxious to release their burdens to the waiting sea roared down hill filling the craters with deadly and impassable water. The valley was now no longer a pathway, but a maze, a maze to which only Jorge and his men had the key. The narrow valley had become a killing ground...and every metre of it had long since been mapped.

The true killing began.

Men already dazed and struggling through the newly formed mud were shot. They were mortared, and they were machine gunned and bombed. There was no mercy shown, for none could be shown. This was a new nation fighting for its right to exist.

Those Fascists who survived the man-made carnage drowned.

Quickly in water if they were lucky. Slowly and more cruelly in the thick grasping mud if they were not.

Jorge could show no pity and though the tears ran down his face and every instinct screamed out against it he kept his mouth firmly closed until nothing stirred in the long valley.

His nation was safe, at least for now. He had not defeated the enemy, only crushed a part of him. It would take months for the enemy to regain his strength. The war here would degrade into raid and counter raid and he had no fear of that. He and his men had bought the fledgling Asturian Republic that which it needed most of all.

Time.

His men raised a thin cheer as he began to walk through them. They loved him, these thin ragged men, they thought of him as one of their own. He gave them encouraging words, promising them better rations and better weapons.

As the sun began to yield to fell night and darkness began to hide the horrors of the battlefield Jorge began a solitary walk hoping that no one saw his tears. He had done what needed to be done, he had used his talent to overcome a more numerous enemy and killed them in uncountable numbers. He wondered if his ancestor had felt this way after destroying the French all those years ago. His grandmother's tales spoke only of death and glory, heroism was mentioned, but the agonies of guilt, of simple survival were not.

He let the tears fall, far away from sight, and then when there were no more tears to shed he walked back to the scene of his victory.

He had won a battle, but there were others still to win. He had sheared the spear point from the enemy's hands, but there were other hands and other spear points. Less powerful hands and smaller, less sharp spears to be sure, but they must be defeated each in turn. He still had neither white horse nor magic cannon, but he'd gladly exchange both for new boots and more bullets.

Perhaps though this was a day to count blessings and not ask for further miracles. He had fought his battle under a sky empty of all but a few enemy aircraft, and though he did not understand why, that was miracle enough.

# FRAGILE PEACE

It had been a very stiff handshake, very stiff indeed and of short duration. But it had pleased his wife and that was something. She had thrust them both out of the house, pleading that the return of her son merited a celebration that needed time and above all space to prepare for. So Georg Maikranz and his son walked the streets in silence, exiled from the neutral territory which almost, though not always, guaranteed civility.

They had no particular destination, no planned route, yet were curiously unwilling to lose sight of each other. Even their footsteps were out of step with each other; Franz had acquired a military step which Georg had long since deliberately forgotten.

Their wanderings had brought them to the very gates of the shipyard where Georg had spent so many hours. He hesitated for a moment, and then without looking to see if he was followed turned through the gates and walked to the great steel warehouse where he was sole master. Faster and faster he walked along the familiar paths, instinctively seeking out the sanctuary.

The sign above his door *Alles ist in ordnung* mocked him though, and he sat at his desk head in his hands, the unwanted emotions swirling and tumbling through his head.

He had not wanted this, this was not what he had sacrificed his life for, starved and gone without for. His son, his sole gift to posterity was to inherit not a uniform and constant danger as he had for five long years but instead comfort and security was to be his inheritance. It had all been arranged over a few glasses of schnapps with the right people; Franz would leave school and then start an apprenticeship here at the shipyards. A safe and secure start to life. What more could any boy want?

Except Franz didn't want a safe and secure life.

What he wanted was to follow the ridiculous idea that he should serve the Fuhrer.

The anger throbbed in his head as the memories returned.

Memories of arguments, of him insisting that his son follow the path chosen for him and of his son refusing to take so much as one step along it. Until one day there were no more arguments, for there was no one to argue with. A post card weeks later announced his son's entry as a boy seaman in the navy and his heart emptied with grief.

There was a soft click as his door opened and he looked up to see the boy...man? , that stood before him.

'Father?' There was a half rueful smile. 'You walk quickly, I could hardly keep up.'

George gave a dismissive grunt. 'I'm not that old; I can move when I need to'.

The conversation ended, and an uncomfortable silence took its place.

'I was wrong'.

Georg looked up at his son, hoping that his words would penetrate the ice that lay between them.

There was no reply, and he was left with no option but to carry on. 'Maybe I was wrong to force you into a trade, maybe you want to do something different. Look how about being a management cadet here? I could pull a few strings, I know I could. It would be difficult, but it could be done. In a few years you could be running your own department, have a pretty secretary making you coffee. How about it, you only signed up as a boy seaman you could still leave and...'

'I've enlisted, father. Ten years.'

'Oh'. The word seemed so inadequate to acknowledge the end of all his hopes for his son's safety and security. He shook his head and tried to resurrect the calm that he was so proud of. 'Does your mother know?'

'Not yet'.

He had to ask the question. 'Why?'

'Because I watched you Father. I watched as you and my mother grew thin, so I could eat what little there was. I watched as you grew grey, as lines appeared on your face. I was a child father, but do you think I didn't see, didn't hear the tears?

'The Fuhrer has promised that those days will not come again, that Germany will be strong again. And she is strong Father, and I will be part of that. That is why.'

Slowly, with much effort George formed his reply. 'But ten years Franz. It will break your mother's heart'.

'And that must never happen Father, we must not let that happen'.

'We?' A little of the old anger returned. 'This is your problem, not mine! You tell her, you wipe her tears!'

'Father it would be better coming from both of us.'

'I'm sure you think so!'

'Father, my mother will be frightened, so you will tell her that I will be safe'.

'And how will I do that?'

'By telling her that I have applied to serve there.' Franz pointed out through the window to where the hull of the battleship already unofficially known as Bismarck was being readied for launching. 'Haven't you repeatedly told mother that she is impregnable, that nothing could sink her? If I am there then in her mind I am safe, it's that simple father. I must follow the Fuhrer, and Germany, Father, just as you followed her in your time.'

A savage memory of blood and bravery, of friends quickly made and quickly lost rose like a deep and painful belch in Georges mind. He fervently wished to save his son from even the remote possibility of gaining similar memories but that was not to be.

'You've applied?'

'Yes Father'.

There was a pause, a hesitation and the rueful smile reappeared. 'Of course I....I may not be accepted'.

'I didn't raise my son to be a failure'. Georg's face was bleak, and his voice was flat, but the comment was a peace overture of sorts. It wasn't acceptance, it wasn't surrender, but recognition that for now, and only for now the war was over.

'Thank you, Father, what do we tell Mother?'

For the first time Georg smiled.

'Tell her? We tell her that you will be buried behind metres of armour plate and will only come up for fresh air and healthy sunshine. We tell her that I personally have selected every centimetre of steel that protects her son and that each and every part of the ship has been made with the express purpose of protecting you and you alone. You on the other hand will tell her that you will take no foolish risks with the life of the son she spent fifteen painful hours delivering, that heroism is the furthest thing on your mind and you will spend your off-duty hours reading improving books and that you will not allow yourself to be dragged into bars...and other places.'

His son raised an eyebrow at this last statement.

'And dammit you will keep a straight face when you say it. You will not have to live with your mother if she worries unduly. I will and believe me it is not a life worth living.' The smile fell from his face. 'It is the very least you can do Franz.'

'Yes father I understand.'

'And finally we tell her that your ship is so powerful, so big, so heavily armoured, has such huge guns that no other ship can compare and therefore your safety is doubly ensured.'

'If you think it best father...and Father?'

'Yes?'

'I really will try not to take risks.'

The words which would condemn his son for placing himself in a position where risks were even a possibility rose unbidden in his mind. He killed them instantly and without passion. They would serve no good purpose now. He and his son had reached a truce, an uneasy, unhappy peace, a peace newly born out of a mutual concern. And perhaps what he had said was not so far from the truth after all. Was it not true that the Bismarck was the last word in warship design? Was it not true that her armour was the best and her guns the most powerful?

Perhaps when he spoke to his wife he would not be lying after all.


The Midshipman's white-collar tabs gleamed softly in the dim light which made a pitiful attempt to illuminate the mess where young Jack McIntyre was trying to sleep.

A slim hand reached out and shook Jack until his eyes were fully open. 'McIntyre? Report to the First Lieutenants office.

'Now sir?'

'Now McIntyre, and for God's sake tidy yourself up, you look like something the cat's dragged in.'

118

With that the midshipman turned on his heels and marched smartly out, leaving Jack to suffer the jibes and catcalls of his fellow boy seamen while trying to make himself presentable before he appeared before the ship's executive officer.

It was a long walk in the pre-dawn gloom that Jack was forced to undertake and as he did so he tried to think just what sin he had committed that would justify being called up at this hour. It must be very bad, as usually any infractions by the boys were dealt with by the petty officers who ran the shore base with rods of iron and the occasional fist.

His heart was beating fast as he stood in the lieutenant's office. The man had acknowledged his presence and then returned to studying the papers that lay before him. At last he looked up and Jack stiffened in response.

'You have completed your gunnery course, McIntyre?

'Yes sir.'

Good conduct awards?

Yes sir, two sir.'

'Above average eyesight I see.'

'Yes sir.'

If there was one thing that Jack had learnt in the Navy it was that no one in his position could go far wrong if he agreed with whatever a senior rank said, he was quite prepared to go on agreeing with the Lieutenant until the sun rose or even until it set for that matter.

'You have applied to join up?'

'Yes sir.'

'Why?'

The question threw him aback for a moment and he tried to marshal his thoughts while the impassive face of the Lieutenant gazed up at him. 'Well sir', Jack's Geordie accent became a little thicker as he tried not to panic, 'It's like this, I grew up around the sea, my dad works in the shipyards and…'

'And?'

Jack could see that the man was testing him, pushing him, seeing if he would stumble.

'And I like the Navy sir, it's fun.' The words came out in a great rush and he knew at that moment that he had failed. The Navy was not supposed to be fun; it was a serious fighting force designed to overawe the enemy or crush him completely. He wondered if he would have time to pack before they threw him through the gates and how he would live from now on.

'Fun?' The man's voice was completely neutral, Jack could detect no approval or disgust with his comment. 'Fun? You think that his Majesty pays you an enormous sum every week to have fun McIntyre, is that what you think? Is that why you have applied to enlist...so you can have fun?'

Jack now knew that his doom was now approaching at full speed and could not be avoided and decided that he would go down unrepentant.

'No sir, it's just that I've learnt a lot and had fun'.

At the last moment his courage almost deserted him and he forced himself to repeat almost inaudibly that he had enjoyed his time as a boy seaman. It sounded inadequate even to him and he waited for the axe to fall.

The lieutenant looked up at the boy who stood in front of him, he'd seen thousands of boys just like this one, many of them products of the slums of the great cities. Three square meals a day, clean clothes, and a shilling or two in their pockets were great inducements to stay on and in his time, he'd heard the boldest lies uttered to him hoping to induce him to sign the paperwork which would allow them to stay on. But every so often he came across boys like this, boys who would with luck rise to become something special. It made his work much less like turning the handle on a sausage machine and more like the vocation he had once believed it to be.

The boy was sweating a little but had stuck to his guns and hadn't backed down.

That showed spirit.

Properly channelled that attitude could aid the Navy.

He allowed his face to adjust itself into what a charitable person would describe as a smile. 'Good!' Truth be told, he enjoyed the look of utter astonishment on the boy's face. There were compensations to rising before the sun, not many to be sure, but this was one of them.

'Sir ?'

'Good, McIntyre, I said good, I'm glad you are having fun, it will make your time in the Navy that much easier.'

A look of puzzlement crossed the boy's face, to be replaced almost instantly by a broad grin as the meaning of his words swiftly penetrated.

'Thank you, sir, thank you very much'.

'Don't thank me McIntyre, thank His Majesty, who is far more charitable than you deserve. Sea time Mr McIntyre, sea time is what you need and I will see that you get it. Report to the movements officer 0930 hours tomorrow for orders.'

Jack was dismissed, but as he was about to leave the sharp voice of the lieutenant called out. 'Good luck Mr McIntyre, and never stop having fun !'


The air had a slight smell of burning charcoal and was filled to capacity with steam that rose in opaque arabesques from the hot rocks that lay far below him.

Leon Blum who lay in a marble tub that was filled with water that was almost, though not quite unbearably hot, sighed and reached out for the damp newspaper. Handling it with care he began to read; he may be out of office, his coalition may have split itself into a thousand squabbling pieces, but he was still a politician and he was still a citizen of France. And what he read disturbed him.

France, his mighty and wayward nation was becoming isolated. The British, thinking to both pacify a rising opposition party and out manoeuvre Germany, had recognised both the forces of General Franco and that of President Tomás in Asturias. A conditional recognition to be sure, but one taken without reference to France, without even so much as a consultation or even a telegram.

Of course the action was a message to his country as well. A message that said plainly that the divisions that had ripped across the face of France must be healed if she was to be considered an equal. A bad situation, but one made worse by the loss of a good friend, who had

121

through the years had always urged greater cooperation with France. With Churchill now condemned to sit far from the centre of power his country had lost a badly needed voice. France it would seem would have to fight her battles alone.

It was time for him to step back into the political ring, the present government was breathing its last breaths and a new election was a certainty.

France must find a new path.

He believed that he could lead France along that path, but in a moment of clarity he saw where that path led and how it would be achieved. And no matter how hard he tried, that thought never failed to depress him.


'Ships company attention!' The Master at Arms voice filled the dockyard.

It was easily heard by Jack McIntyre, who as a mere boy had one hundred and forty-five other people between him and the Captain.

It was a time-honoured tradition of the Navy 'Brass at the front, rabble at the back' as someone once explained it to him. It didn't matter, he could see enough and hear clearly as the captain's voice echoed from the quayside walls.

The Foxhound had been in action once before he knew that, though there was no sign of that to be seen under the newly painted steel. It was obvious that men just as skilled as his father had laboured long and hard to repair the damage caused by the Spanish cruiser. He let his eyes wander to the guns that pointed out over the bow, they looked very impressive and he hoped that one day he might rise high enough to command one of the turrets. Sea time he had been promised and it looked as if he was getting it...and in a crack destroyer too.

Life he decided could not get any better.


'Move your arse, Maikranz!'

Franz's arms and legs did not just ache, they burnt, as muscle and sinew protested at the unaccustomed effort. This was the tenth time he had climbed up the rough hempen rope, and the roof of the gymnasium seemed to reach higher each time.

'Move it I say, by God you'd move fast enough if a British destroyer was after you, now move !'

The instructor, a grey-haired veteran of the Great War gave the end of the rope an encouraging shake, which caused Franz to grip all the tighter and then with a soft groan ascend to the iron girders which marked the end of his journey.

The hard voice floated up to him. 'That took far too long Maikranz, far, far too long; now come down and give me ten laps.'

Franz hated the instructor, they all did. No effort however diligent or well performed seemed to please him. His use of sarcasm bordered on genius and his fists had obviously been fashioned out of iron and teak. Any rebellion was dealt with quickly and efficiently without him raising a sweat, although to do the man justice he did not seem to bear grudges. But this was what Franz had signed up for.

He remembered how happy he had been when he had been accepted for the Bismarck's crew, he remembered his Mothers tears and his Father, white-faced as he was plunged into the unaccustomed role of mediator between the two of them. But he had been accepted and on his first day it was explained to him just how hard his life was to become.

The Bismarck's crew were to be the best in the navy, there was to be no half-hearted efforts, no slacking, only a one hundred per cent effort would be acceptable, and that was to be so not just when on duty, but at all times.

Franz had not believed them, he was devoted to Germany and the Fuhrer, but such an intense effort was surely impossible. Weeks later his disbelief had entirely eroded away. The failure rate was high and many a man and more than a few boys had made the long walk to the main gate never to be seen again.

Franz re- doubled his efforts and his nights were spent studying seamanship, navigation, damage control, gunnery, the thousand and one things that were demanded of him. Exams, tests and courses filled his days and every exam and every test had its failed candidates which left Franz as part of a rapidly diminishing group. Every day brought him closer to breaking point, every night brought him nearer to failure.

Yet he could not break and he could not fail. How could he fail the Fuhrer who had done so much for Germany? The thought, the very idea was impossible to contemplate. Yet there was another thought and another motivation which hid in the recesses of his mind. If he failed he would have to face his father.

And that was an interview he was not willing to take.


There would be no war of that he was certain.

Neville Chamberlain would not turn round, he would not show fear, he would not show annoyance or any other emotion. He would not face his tormentor, who stood just feet behind him. Instead he concentrated on the ornate mace that sat on the table before him. It too was unmoved as the voice grew every more grave and the barbs grew ever more pointed.

The House of Commons was full of course, and why wouldn't it be? Churchill had asked the Speaker of the House for leave to speak, to tell the House just why he resigned. They were murmuring now, just barely audible, a soft susurration not unlike the sound a field of wheat would make before a summer storm rode through it. And that is what this was; a summer storm to be endured and to be withstood.

There would be no war. He would not go down in history as the man who led his country and its empire into a war. Whatever the red-faced man behind him said he would steer any course which led away from that awful abyss. Yet as Churchill's voice filled the air the murmurs became louder, and disturbingly some of them were from his own side. He lifted his eyes from the gilded and bejewelled mace and risked a quick glance across the table.

Atlee was, as he expected showing no emotion at all, for all Churchill's oratory and passion he might have been listening to a weather report. Wilkinson was barely suppressing a wide grin. He was certain that she would be claiming the credit for this split in his cabinet. He offered up a silent prayer to God that he remove the woman but he suspected that miracles of that magnitude would be in short supply.

124

Churchill's voice continued on; warning, cajoling and offering dire predictions of dire fates. Then with a final burst of eloquence the speech ended.

There was silence for a moment as the last words were absorbed into the fabric of the chamber, then a series of shouts of approval. They were loud, but he judged there were not enough of them. There would be no fatal split in his party, no grand alliance between the Labour right wing and Churchill's true believers.

But above all, there would be no war.


Atlee kept his face perfectly still during Churchill's speech; not by so much as a raised eyebrow would he show any sign of approval, or for that matter disapproval.

Had Ellen's campaign pushed Churchill to set fire to the tent he had for so long wished to enter? He was unsure.

Ellen certainly thought so, but he had his doubts; the tensions between the Prime Minister and Churchill had been evident even to the most obtuse ever since the Foxhound incident.

He was certain of one thing. There could be no alliance, formal or informal with Churchill and his band of followers. To do so would discredit and very likely split his party, and besides any attempt to do so may very well drive the man back into the Tory heartland. No, it was better to remain on good terms with both men and watch while the Prime Minister fought both his own Labour Party and an embittered Churchill.

A two front war was now the only option for the grey-moustached man. He was certain that Chamberlain had noticed just how uneasy some of his own backbencher's were during the speech and that would be an additional burden for him to carry. All of these stresses and strains would weaken the Conservatives and make his work a little easier. They had come so close last time and the next election could see them sweep into power and enshrine him as the first Prime Minister to lead a wholly Labour government.

A small burst of happy anticipation bubbled through him but was never revealed on his face. He was looking forward to that next election.

1940 was going to be a good year.

# REBIRTH

It was the tide that decided just when she would be released and one particular day when the moon was in the right quarter was deemed the most auspicious.

But who was to free her?

The question rolled through Jarrow endlessly.

The celebration was to be the biggest and best Jarrow had ever seen, every town and city that had contributed so much as a tin of paint or a brass screw had been invited to the ceremony.

But who would launch her, who would release the Hood from her captivity? The Mayor perhaps or one of the councillors? Perhaps Ellen Wilkinson herself or another politician? Maybe the King himself would arrive in state and release the greatest ship in his Navy?

The answer though was obvious.


Pulver sat in the command chair on the Hood's bridge, a bank of telephones in front of him and a naval rating at his side. The Navy had insisted on having a 'Naval presence' on board when the Hood was re-floated, though if he was honest if anything went wrong there was little he could do. So he sat in a very comfortable chair that was set into the floor of a new designed bridge and watched as the ceremonies began.

There were speeches of course, everyone who had been in any way involved with the Hood seemed to think that fact gave them permission to bore everyone else.

Jarrow had spared no expense today, bunting by the mile and flags by the hundred whipped and fluttered in the breeze.

There was food and drink enough to feed multitudes and Pulver chewed reflectively on a ham sandwich that he had liberated before boarding his ship.

The last speech ended and the last toast was drunk and a short man in an ill-fitting and obviously new suit walked up to the great wheel that would allow the waiting sea her long delayed entry.

There was silence now as he placed his hands on the rim of the wheel and began to turn it.

And stopped.

Shaking his head he ran back into the crowd and dragged an obviously protesting Mabel McIntyre and her two daughters back with him to the great wheel.

Carefully placing each set of hands on the wheel he nodded and together they all began to turn the wheel which began turn faster and faster.

A great buzz of laughter and approval ran through the crowd.

Jarrow had chosen well. The Hood had been rebuilt not just by the sweat of men alone, but by the grit and determination of women like Mabel McIntyre.

Pulver saw the flash of a re-bought wedding ring on Mabel's finger and was about to comment when the Hood began to gently tremble.

His ship was being reborn.


She never saw the hands that turned the valves, but she felt the effects as the brackish water began touching her with a thousand whispering fingers.

She heard the sea's siren voice calling her, challenging her, reproaching her for her long absence.

She began to float, lifting off the blocks; an inch then six, then with a great heave she was free and a wave of debris stained water was thrown from her.

The great wooden props, their duty done fell into the water and floated dolefully away.

She was free.

She trembled, every plate every, frame and strake vibrating with delight. Never had the breeze been so scented, never had the sun shone so brightly.

A hundred joyful songs ran through her.

She was free.

The great gates of the dry dock swung open and her friends pushed, pulled and prodded her to her fitting out berth.

Work hardened hands pulled her tight to the wharf.

The sea uplifted her and made her welcome.

She was free.

'Who are you ?'

The words woke them from their long slumber. Bright moonlight threw soft shadows across all of them, but they could not see who spoke.

The voice had power in it, and authority. It was not a voice to be ignored, yet there was no malice in it. 'Who are you ?'

The voice had no focus, it seemed to come from everywhere at once.

They looked again but saw nothing.

Finally the bravest of them spoke. 'If you please, we are four point five inch dual purpose guns.'

Another broke in. 'Yes we are, and we can fire all sorts of shells.'

There was a babble of voices now.

'Yes we can fire armour piercing and anti-aircraft.'

'Star shell don't forget star shell!'

'And shrapnel, I like shrapnel.'

'Yes and we can fire for miles and miles.'

'And quickly too.'

'Yes, ever so quickly'.

They fell silent, a little embarrassed by their sudden enthusiasm.

There was a hint of amusement in the voice now. 'And how far can you throw your shells?'

The brave one spoke with pride. 'Nearly eleven miles.'

A soft chuckle fell from one of the fifteen-inch mouths of 'A' turret which hurt the brave ones feelings. A tiny shade of anger passed through him. 'And who are you......who are you to question us?'

'I am the Hood', came the reply. 'I am every rivet, every plate and much more.

128

'I am the sweat and blood of my makers and of the men who gave me new life.

'I am my crew, their passions and their cares.

'I am calm seas and rough waves.

'I am safe harbours and far away ports.

'I am ice and sunshine.

'I am duty and service.

'I am the Hood…and I have been re born.'

There was obviously no answer to the statement and the new recruits waited in the moonlight for the Hood to continue.

The contralto voice caressed them, washing them with warmth. 'So my children who can throw shells nearly eleven miles very, very quickly what will you do if I am threatened? Will you remain silent and unused? Will you remain idle while I am beset with enemies?'

The recruits shouted with one voice.

'No! We'll bite!

'And scratch!

'And kick!

'And punch!

'We won't let anyone hurt you!'

The Hood's voice trembled with pleasure. 'I am pleased that you think so, and that you are now part of me, may we serve long together. Now my children, tomorrow you shall begin, and this is what you must do…'

Together the new recruits listened.

They were part of her now.

# THE LAST OF THE PEACE

The city of light was undoubtedly a beautiful city but tonight its lights, its wide boulevards and its impressive architecture were hidden under a thick blanket of snow. It was a different kind of beauty and Leon Blum was impervious to it. He was back in the race, back in power.

The last government had followed so many others in France's history and fallen unable to withstand the stresses of the time.

Czechoslovakia had fallen before German might and in dying had, almost as a last act fired a poison dart not at Germany, but at her traitorous friend, France.

A cabinet minister had taken that dart and resigned.

But that was only the beginning.

Georges Mandel, a rising political star had not just resigned over the betrayal of France's ally and the soiling of her honour, but had resigned publicly, noisily and with bitter, bitter words. It was a blow that no government, even a stable one could survive and the French public relieved that war had been averted was asked to pay the price by going once more to the polling booths.

Enough of them, and if he was honest only just enough of them, trusted Leon Blum, and trusted him to keep them at peace whatever happened, whatever ill wind blew.

But all around him lay wreckage.

The wreckage of failed governments.

The wreckage of failed policies that were born only to be murdered by succeeding governments.

And linking these disasters like a grisly daisy chain were missed chances and the debris of opportunities foolishly ignored.

It was a daunting task he had set himself.

He had been told that a good mechanic could repair any machine and a master mechanic could assemble useful and productive items out of almost nothing. He had no experience with tools and even the poorest mechanic would look upon him with scorn, yet he must imitate not the poor mechanic, nor even the good mechanic, but

130

must jump straight into the shoes of the master mechanic and fabricate a working machine out of the men that France had long since discarded.

He began to run his eyes down a list of names, seeking to balance left and right, seeking to place men in positions where they could do the most good, or at least the minimum harm. A cabinet must be built that represented all of France and he could already hear the cries of outrage that would that would echo from every quarter.

To build a government that had within it both right and left was an almost impossible task, yet as he looked at the map of Europe that hung on the wall he knew that an even harder one awaited him.

For France must fight, and fight before it was impossible to fight, before her only option was to fight with no hope of victory. But not on the sacred soil of France where a generations blood had been shed and leached away much of her strength. Her battles must be fought elsewhere, away from her weary people and open defenceless cities.

He turned his eyes from a long list of failed politicians and looked at a map of France and her neighbours. The map was an old one, drawn when the angel of peace ruled with smiles and bright light, but now a far different angel ruled the world.

France needed secure borders and allies she could control.

And there was one place where such things could be found.

Asturias.


'How long ?'

Jorge looked at the nervous men who sat before him.

These were the men who ruled the Asturian Republic, who had read out the proclamation that announced its birth. And these men more than any others had the most to lose.

'You ask how long?'

Jorge undid the wide belt that held together the half-cured sheepskin coat that had become his own personal trade mark and walked over to the blackboard. Quickly he drew a crude map of Spain. He knew he was no artist, his schooling had been of short duration and had not given him much time for self-expression, but he had learnt valuable lessons over the past year and he intended to teach these educated men a little of what blood and battle had taught him.

He stabbed at the board with a chalk stick which instantly crumbled under the pressure. 'Our victories here in the North have forced the Nationalists to move South...and they have been successful. Madrid will fall soon, nothing is more certain. Once that happens Franco and his bastards have won.

'There may still be resistance, but effectively the war is over. Germany and Italy will recognise him as a legitimate winner, so will France and so will the British, reluctantly, but they will do so. Moscow will retreat and lick her wounds; we can expect no more help from her.

'When that happens, once the Nationalists have the whole of the South, once the arrests have been made and the firing squads have finished their work, then they will come back here. It won't be through the mountains this time. They have learnt their lesson; ten thousand graves have taught them well. No, this time they will come by sea.'

He drew great sweeping arrows on the crude map. Each and every one of them stabbed the northern coastline.

'We have no effective navy; the Basques are even worse off with only a few armed trawlers still in operation. When the British recognise Franco their navy will leave our coast and the Fascists will come straight down our throats'.

There was a protest, a protest born of fear and disbelief.

'But we have an army, and you have defeated them before!'

Jorge heard the educated voice, heard the fear in it and wondered how to explain just how few miracles he had left to perform. He had no difficulty making his voice sound grave, this was not a time for jesting.

'Yes, we have an army. An army that is trained to fight from ambush. An army that is few in number, armed with captured weapons. We have an air force that flies aircraft that can barely support themselves in the air'.

He looked on knowing they did not understand.

'And where would you have me put my army? Must I defend Gijón, is that what I must do? If I must, then what if the enemy lands here, or here?'

His hand moved in savage arcs across the board, each movement leaving a white chalky sign of death.

'How then do I move my men, my equipment? This time I must move towards the enemy on a ground of their choosing, not mine.' He shrugged, and his face registered resignation. 'I will be defeated. In one battle or ten, it doesn't matter, the end will be the same.

'So you ask me how long. Snow is falling in the mountains now and we are safe for the winter. Franco will take that time to swallow what is left of Spain. That is how long. By spring when the snows melt and the air clears it will begin.

'I've bought you time. If you want to live, if you want our nation to live, find a way to stop Franco that does not depend on bullets or bayonets'.

The white faces stared at him.

He felt pity for them; it had taken courage to declare nationhood, to say to Spain and the world that they would stand and stand alone. Not that they had much choice about it, but still courage was courage and took many forms and though he had the typical peasant disdain for intellectuals he could still recognise valour when he saw it. It might take some encouragement, even a little pushing, but the courage still existed.

He came to a decision and let go of the harshness in his voice and adopted a softer tone. He did not have the words to explain what was in his mind and for a moment he struggled to find a way to describe what he saw.

He smiled for a brief moment as the memory rose up of a day long ago and a girl he once knew. He let the smile shine on the men and began. 'We are like the ugly girl at the village dance. We sit by the door looking at every arrival with hope, but no one wants to dance with us. That is our problem gentlemen, our possible dance partners do not like the way we dance, they do not like the way we live, they fear us for what we are. But we are in luck; there is an even uglier girl, and unlike us she does not wait for the soft hand that will lift her to her feet. This girl dances with many and when she has finished with them they are never the same.'

He turned again to the roughly drawn map and carefully drew a great cross through it.

'The dance here is nearly over and many fear that they will be the one who is forced to dance with her next.'

He paused a little before his next words. 'Perhaps they would rather dance with us. Perhaps the dance will be brief. But perhaps they may find that a girl like us is less of a threat. Perhaps we can make the very ugly girl a little bit cautious, even a little bit jealous. But to woo these suitors we must make ourselves pretty and lose a little of what has made us ugly in their eyes. A new dress, a little make up and we are transformed'.

He knew there would be an explosive reaction to his suggestion and he was not disappointed; there was a babble of angry voices.

'No!'

'Never!'

'You would ask us to surrender!'

'What about the principles of the revolution!'

'You would turn us into all we hate!'

Jorge's smile vanished and the military man returned. The harsh voice of the battlefield filled the room. 'I would ask you to survive, no more than that. Keep your principles keep your beliefs but walk softly if you would seek allies. My men bled and died, held the mountain passes for you. They weren't afraid to die for Asturias....are you?'

A malevolent devil entered his mind and directed his next words. 'Imagine gentlemen that the Nationalists have won. They enter this room, there are blows, many blows, each more painful that the last. Then there is the prison cell, damp and uncomfortable. You are hungry and thirsty.

'Then after a trial in which insults are heaped upon you there is the execution. Can you feel the rope around your neck, feel your lungs begging for air? That awaits you if you lose.'

White faces turned even whiter. These were educated men and his words had more effect here than they would on his own rough-hewn men.

'Dance or die those are your only choices, make your choice and make it soon'.

He left the room, angrily stalking out, while behind him the voices rose and fell.

He had said what was in his heart and there was no more that could be said. He hoped it would be enough. He needed time now, time to let a little serenity return to his soul.

And time to plan a spring campaign that he knew could only end in defeat.


Aspiring officers of the Royal Navy simply did not read the Daily Mirror, so this was a guilty pleasure that happened every Saturday morning.

Pulver sat up in bed, his unshaven face covered in toast crumbs and the last traces of two soft boiled eggs.

The Mirror had swung behind Attlee's push for rearmament with gusto and if that meant printing excerpts from Churchill's speeches then it would do so...if only to expose divisions within the Tory party.

He swept the crumbs from the paper and read Churchill's gloomy and biting comments about the annexation of Sudetenland. '*A defeat of the first order*' and '*Czechoslovakia recedes into darkness*' were coupled with '*A catalogue of grievous errors and false assumptions*' and '*This government has been weighed in the balance and has been found wanting.*'

It all made very sad and indeed alarming reading, and what made it worse was the fact that Pulver knew very few Navy officers who did not subscribe to Churchill's views. It was a shame he thought that the government was not in the habit of consulting junior lieutenants because he was of the same opinion as the heretical M.P and his growing band of followers. War was coming and only a fool would believe otherwise.

A bitter brew was being prepared and the nation stood with resignation and prepared to drink again from a cup they had hoped they would never have to touch again.

There was only one bright light on a rapidly darkening horizon, he had been promised…well half-promised at least, that he would serve on the Hood when she commissioned. A war on the Hood and a Hood faster and more powerful than ever before was a prize that eclipsed any thought of danger or even leaving the owner of those grey-green eyes.

He stirred and reluctantly got out of bed. Hurrying to the coal fire he placed several lumps of Welsh anthracite on the flames which were doing their best to combat an unusually cold late autumn.

He dived back into the rapidly cooling bed and saying farewell to Churchill and politics turned to the real reason he bought the Daily Mirror. Jane was a barely clothed cartoon character, whose adventures always seemed to involve her losing what little clothing she had. If he was honest Jane was the real reason Pulver bought the Daily Mirror.

Politicians, wars even nations may come and go.

But Jane always gave satisfaction.


Warmth, the Hood felt warmth

A gentle beating warmth.

Then heat.

Hot savage heat that turned steam into a leashed monster.

Her hearts, newer and better than before began to beat.

Slowly.

Oh so slowly.

She felt the steam rush down pipes, its joy of release frustrated as it discovered that escape must ever be at a price.

Turbines laughed and began to spin, turning the great drive shafts that dully reflected every gantry light.

Slowly they turned.

Oh so slowly.

Sluggishly the muddy water in which she lay began to churn.

Slowly.

Oh so slowly.

Bearings, stiff in their housings complained, then settled down to their tasks.

Thrust blocks grunted as they pushed back against tons of phosphor bronze propeller.

And then it was over.

The turbines laughter turned to a diminishing giggle and then to silence.

The shafts turned no more and the propellers became calm and inert.

She knew that there would time later for her hearts to beat faster, fast enough for her to race through the water, but today her friends were satisfied.

And so was she.


The oil had been fed into the boilers with care.

Pulver had noted the fact with approval. Only a fool would overheat new boilers - burst pipes and smashed manifolds would surely follow such an act and the men from Jarrow were no fools.

All day the boilers had been fed. Drop by increasing drop. This was not the day for a high pressure run. That day lay in the future. This day had its own pleasures and its own perils. This was the day that The Hoods new hearts would beat for the first time.

He reached out and placed an oil stained hand on a burnished copper pipe, murmuring what he hoped were comforting words to his ship, assuring her that this was but a beginning, that the day was not far off when her hearts would throb with power and that her power would then be given full release. 'Be patient old girl, we'll walk a little before you run, then you'll show them. But not today. Soon though old girl, soon.'

His hand left the pipe leaving five delicate impressions of his fingerprints on the pipe which gradually blurred as the pipe warmed. They remained there as a link between him and the Hood as he walked away and watched as valves were opened with delicacy. Steam was released, travelling not where it wished, but where it was needed. There was movement now, slow and at first heart-stoppingly hesitant. The turbines began to whine as they sought to overcome the weight of the great drive shafts and the new cunningly crafted propellers.

The cavernous spaces began to fill with a subdued roar as machinery flashed into life. Electricity flowed, steam lines creaked as steam sought urgent release, a thousand separate noises, a thousand separate voices that blended into a great symphony of power.

Pulver grinned with joy.

The Hood had a heartbeat.

Now she was truly alive.

And soon, very, very soon she would begin her sea trials.


'We,' she was told,' are the subject of no less than thirty-six separate patents, six of them still on the secret list. Our main bearings, of which there are over fifty in every one of us cost in excess of twenty-five pounds each and even the meanest of our gears has been machined from the finest bronze to previously unheard of tolerances. We can without any effort at all do over thirty calculations at the same time.'

The dry voices were just a little stilted, and oddly enough reminded her of chalk dust and blackboards.

These were the new Fire control computers who would rule the fifteen-inch guns and the four point five inch guns who now ringed her.

She smiled a little at the thought of her boisterous new children being ruled by the pedantic voices which came from deep within her. Perhaps a quiet word with them later would be wise.

Truthfully, she missed the old firing computer. Despite his bumbling inaccuracy she liked him. These new members of her team however seemed all too sure of themselves. Managing her gruff old guns and her new recruits was a job which would require tact, understanding and above all patience. All that she suspected would take time, and she was beginning to ask herself just how much time she had.

Because from far across the oceans she was beginning to hear the beat of drums.

# A RUN TO WAR

The coffee lay cold and un-drunk before him, a sandwich, despairing of ever fulfilling its purpose had begun to curl its arms towards the ornate ceiling. Leon Blum stared vacantly up towards it. The doubts warred in his head like contending titans.

He had tried, but was it enough? Had the effort been worthwhile? He could not tell.

Right and left had sought to tear at each other and those who occupied the thin middle ground.

His skill had allied with his cunning and each bomb had been diffused before it could explode and rip his fragile government into rags and tatters.

He had handed out carrots like a demented greengrocer and used the stick with reluctance and discretion when bribery and compromise failed.

Against his instincts, against his beliefs he had held the centre.

And held it still.

Against the odds.

Against all those who said he would fail and those who wished he would fail.

He had held.

Held for France, for the bleeding, wounded land the loved.

But had it been enough? Had he made the right choices? The questions haunted and harried him late into the night. Each appointment, every decision, every announcement his government had made was done to reassure France, to apply bandages to her wounds or at the very least paper over the cracks.

But every one of them had a second purpose. They sent a message that France now had a direction, and resolve, that though she wished ardently for peace and would do all within her power to keep it she had drawn a line.

And yet there was still the fear that the line would be crossed so the new-found resolve had a dash of caution in it.

France's strength would be placed at her edges, great and expensive fortifications would hold the eastern door to his country firmly closed. And yet there were other doors to France and those doors could not be barred, for the key lay not in their hands but in other, envious hands.

But even there a solution could be found. Far to the South lay the last flickering flame of resistance to all that he found hateful, all that France feared. Yet it was a red flame that glimmering cast its baleful glare across the Pyrenees and there were those in France who would not be sorry if it were extinguished. The Asturians had been allowed to live so that they might be a source of division and infection within the body of his country.

They were a living knife plunged deep within her. And yet it was a poor knife that could not be turned on its owner and Blum had with care and great fear extracted the weapon and re fashioned it.

It had been his greatest test for he had brought down upon his head the wrath of many. His own left wing attacked him for using the Asturians who had committed the cardinal sin of breaking away from Moscow. This was the central tenet of their religion and they had howled in anger. Yet to aid communists, anarchists and left wingers was a bitter draught for the right wing of his government to swallow. In their world there were no shades of red and they too had screamed with outrage.

Only political reality and patriotism had aided him.

Spain was still weak, but Madrid had already begun took look about her and cast covetous eyes upon France Outré la Mer. A second Spanish empire could be hers with Tuareg and Berber taking the place of Inca and Aztec. That day could be far off but it would be better if it never came at all.

So the Asturians gave solemn assurances and would become watchmen. Madrid would be forced to look north and not across the Mediterranean. French aid trickled south along narrow and winding coast roads, slowly and in frustratingly small amounts. Her watchmen were not what she would wish for and they received less than they wanted, yet they must do their duty as best they may.

It was a compromise and like all compromises pleased no one.

France had muttered and writhed with unease at this move, but gradually the muttering became less audible and the unease became part of the background of events. His government had survived, and France, could now breathe a little easier, but only a little.

He sighed, the pain of those battles still fresh in his memory, picked up the coffee cup and instantly rejected the frigid brew and dismissed the dry sandwich. He looked at them for a few moments and wondered how much more he could ask of the French people. They were undoubtedly brave but were still scarred from war and wished ardently that the sacrifices of the last generation would not be repeated.

They trusted him to pull the rabbit of peace out of the hat of war each and every day. They trusted him with their lives.

He walked to the window and looked out over Paris, peaceful, beautiful Paris. A delayed spring had left pale green buds on the trees and even at this late hour lovers still walked hand in hand beneath them. A couple stopped and exchanged a kiss and though the kiss was chaste the girl fell into the man's arms, surrendering to him in a moment's passion.

And that was all it took, he could resist no longer.

He groaned and put his head in his hands, the truth which he had been fending off had stormed the walls and now stood grinning triumphantly before him. He knew that the man would soon be called to the colours and she, if she was lucky, would write tear-stained letters to him while sheltering in a damp cellar.

He had known it, and he had known from the start.

It wasn't enough, all his efforts the compromises, the statements, the deals, good and bad, were all in vain.

Because one day soon he knew that he would pull not a rabbit out of the hat.

Soon his hand would pull out a different object.

A sword.


'A little less mortar Mr Ambassador'. Churchill's voice came through a cloud of morning mist and cigar smoke.

René Massigli grimaced as he pushed down on the rough brick, and, as predicted the mortar oozed out like the cream from a chocolate éclair.

A good-natured grin escaped from the cigar smoke.

'It takes practice, that I do admit; allow me.'

Two deft strokes of a trowel were applied and the excess mortar was removed. The brick, looking a good deal more respectable was now joined with hundreds of its brothers.

Despite his amateur efforts Massigli was well pleased with his attempts, though this was not why he was spending the weekend at Chartwell.

Another brick was added and Churchill took the opportunity to open the conversation that Massigli had been wishing for. 'I do hope you are not going to ask me to speak in favour of your policy in Spain'.

Massigli was not surprised at the comment. He knew that asking the man to support any left-wing cause was an exercise in futility, so he returned Churchill's grin and wiped his hands on the proffered towel. 'My dear Mr Churchill I would not ask such a thing of you. Besides…' he added with just a touch of levity, '…your own Labour Party is carrying out that task quite adequately.'

A grunt escaped from the cigar smoke. 'Yes. A damn fine job they are making of it but Chamberlain won't budge. He believes that he can still manage Hitler and maintain peace. Every new bomber we build, every new keel we lay down he views as a personal attack'.

Massigli nodded sadly. 'And yet the man is sincere in his beliefs. He does not act the part. He really does believe that Germany is now content.'

The cigar flared into angry life. 'And that makes it much harder. I cannot pierce that sincerity, and your government's actions in Spain have put him under severe pressure. How can he recognise Franco as leader when you insist that the whole question of Northern Spain is still under debate? The more you push him the more fixed he becomes.'

Churchill's voice became exasperated. 'I'm damned if I know why he became a politician in the first place, he hates politics and lacks that essential element of any politician.'

'Compromise,' added Massigli softly. 'We too have found it so. It has made my life a little difficult.'

Churchill's face softened, the anger falling away. He knew full well that Massigli's position as ambassador was not only new, but highly precarious. The man had many enemies, and only political power was keeping him in place. There were many in France who looked across the Rhine for allies, rather than towards the west, and more than a few of those inhabited the French foreign ministry.

Massigli's appointment was a visible sign that Paris, or at least elements within the French government wished for closer ties with London.

'I wish I could do more', he said, genuine regret in his voice. 'I will of course continue to push for greater cooperation between our nations.'

'Except over Spain, my dear Winston?' For just a second the polite diplomatic mask faded.

'Except over Spain...' agreed Churchill. '...and if I'm honest I too have misgivings over the whole affair. There are some who say that Spain is a distraction which will dilute French efforts that should by right go elsewhere.'

There was a very Gallic shrug from the diplomat and a humourless smile ran across his face. 'It is a choice we have made. We would much have preferred for you to have made the same choice but there are other paths where we may walk together. And besides Asturias is such a little line in the sand, such a small portion of our power that in the long run we risk little. If the Asturians win, then Franco is weakened and if they lose then his enmity will hardly be increased, and France will have lost very little that would not have been lost had we done nothing.'

'A penny ticket in a lottery', agreed Churchill. 'And the Asturians, they know this, they know they are a disposable commodity?'

Again there was a shrug with just a hint of cynicism. 'That was not our concern, besides they were hardly in a position to argue.'

The cynicism did not disturb Churchill. The strong had always dominated the weak, and that applied just as much to international relations as to any other sphere so he made a gesture of understanding and allowed Massigli to continue.

'We have made our move and made our intentions plain. We hope that Herr Hitler will draw the correct conclusion. But though we have moved a pawn our position with regards to your country remains the same. We look for closer ties and joint moves to limit German expansionism, and I look to you and your contacts to aid me in my task'.

From there the conversation ranged far and wide. Poland, the Soviet Union, America, the Balkans, all were eagerly discussed, Churchill's free ranging imagination tempered by the Frenchman's more sardonic personality. Bricks were forgotten as the sun rose higher and higher; ideas, possibilities were made, discarded and adapted.

Only hunger halted the discussion and both men walked up to the house and dressed for lunch.

Here the conversation was a little lighter and Churchill was regaling his guests with a tales of his time in America when a telegram was delivered.

Churchill read it and gave a surprised grunt. 'It seems Mr ambassador that Herr Hitler has most carefully considered your move in Spain, considered it most carefully indeed. And here is his response'. He turned to Massigli and handed him the telegram.

It was a short telegram, just a few words but as he read them their import became instantly apparent and the single sheet of paper dropped from shocked fingers.

That morning while bricks were being laid, while plans were discussed the German army had moved.

What was left of Czechoslovakia was now no more.


Jorge was still a little shocked at the sight.

There were one hundred and forty of them and they were the second most beautiful things he had seen this week.

They were old that was true, but they were reliable and were, best of all, proven killers. The French cannons were Great War *seventy fives* and each one had arrived, towed by a modern truck. Now he had mobile artillery and some very disreputable French gunners who had assured him that they were all volunteers with no links whatsoever to the French government.

He had shrugged. Such things did not concern him, so long as they could lay guns fast and accurately and obey orders then he would be content.

The guns were a great gift and very useful, but he had lost his heart to the occupants of a small warehouse that lay at the edge of docks.

Boots.

Thirty thousand boots, each and every one of them harder than a harlot's heart. And each and every one of them dearer to him than anything else.

Even now the women were rubbing sheep fat into them restoring their suppleness. Once the women were finished his men would have boots capable of withstanding anything that the Spanish roads could throw at them.

Now he could march and hit.

Now he must wait for the blow to fall.


Neville Chamberlain looked again at the speech he was to give. Every line radiated hope for the future and a belief in peace. The speech was to be a testament to the logic and force of his policies.

And every word was false.

Every line.

Every comma.

Every paragraph.

All lied.

His hopes, his beliefs, the very foundations of his life and his political creed had been shattered today. Today, the day when Hitler destroyed what was left of Czechoslovakia was the day when his eyes were opened and he saw Hitler in a new light and not the light that his hopes had shone on the man. A white-hot anger roared through him and he reached for the papers, his hands ready to tear the speech into shreds.

And stopped.

The doctor had advised against excesses and ripping the paper to shreds surely came under that category.

He pushed away the sadness and the anger and drawing on the steel core of his mind which had served him well since boyhood, he picked up fresh sheets of paper and began to write anew. There would be war now, despite all his efforts, despite all the slights and insults he had endured. Very well he would, if God spared him lead his country into war.

He began to write the melancholy words he knew his people were hoping not to hear.


There was no single instant when she was born.

The shock of her launching failed to push her to full consciousness as did the fitting of the first of her long-barrelled guns.

It was a gradual thing this waking.

Uncounted footsteps, a million exertions tiny and great.

A bolt tightened with a satisfied grunt, a splash of paint in just the right place, all these and many others accumulated and added to what she was.

Gradually she swam towards the light, groping her way along unfamiliar corridors and strange shapes.

There were questions and unknowns that must be answered, but first she must find herself a name.

She listened intently to the men who scurried within and without her, straining to hear a name, any name.

There was one word spoken above all others and it seemed to fit, moulding itself around her like a warm cloak.

She decided that this name was her, this was what she was, what she would become, what she would always be.

She was Bismarck.

And was born in that instant.

Born to rule.


The Hood had been pulled down the channel by two tugs who had been burnished to a soft glow in honour of the occasion, but once

146

free of the land they had cast off their lines and were now faint wisps of smoke on the horizon.

The red and white lighthouse that would mark the beginning of her run was just in sight. Uncounted months of work, uncounted drops of blood and sweat had led to this point. Difficulties without number had been vanquished, decisions made and remade before the Hood had felt true sea water under her keel. And now all that skill and effort was to be put to the test. This was her first sea run, one of many she would perform under the blood red phoenix flag of Palmer's Shipyard.

The sky was grey, the sea restless, but still the Hood moved.

Fast.

Faster.

No wave could resist her, each and every one was split and sundered.

Fast.

Faster.

The wind battered at her, seeking in vain to enter her proud new bridge, but she ignored every surge of damp air.

Faster.

Yet faster.

She ran through the water, turning sharply this way and that, obeying every command with speed and grace. Her guns turned and raised, smoke poured from her funnels, machinery was tested up to the very limits of its endurance. Anxious men grew calmer as it became obvious that the Hood had been truly transformed. No longer was she the tired warrior doing her duty with worn muscles and creaking ligaments.

Now she was the Hood, reborn.

Fast.

Faster.

The wave burst over her in a welter of spray and rainbows and vanished.

'Welcome'.

The next wave was smashed by her steel bow.

'Back '.

A wave rose and fell.

'We've…'

A wave cunningly tried to climb her sides but was repulsed.

'Missed…'

Her stern was slammed down onto the receptive sea.

'You!'

She rose up and gave a joyful half roll.

'I'm back', she replied. 'I am the Hood and I'm back'.

'We know, we know, we know,' the waves answered, their salty voices whipped by the wind. 'You are the Hood and we have missed you, have you missed us?'

'More than I can say'.

A wave slapped her with a foam-fringed hand.

'Then let's play!'


'We really are very sorry'. The voice was doleful and more than a little upset.

A steam line had burst, loudly and explosively. The newly escaped steam had hung damp and dissipating, trading insults with the outraged lines until it and its insults faded away. The steam lines exuded unhappiness as they continued their tale. 'We thought we could hold, and we were trying really hard, but at the last minute the stream just pushed out. We really are very sorry. We do hope no one was hurt'.

The steam lines gloom hung in the air just as the steam had done.

The Hood was about to intervene and give soothing words of encouragement but before she could do so the turbines broke the spell.

The turbines were always excessively cheerful, which she always thought unusual considering they spent their lives rotating at speeds which made her giddy when she thought of it, but today it was they and not her who rescued the lines from their despair.

'Well the steam was jolly rude we must say and said some rather unpleasant things, but we did laugh at your replies'.

'You did?'

Oh yes, we particularly liked your *failed fog* and *dismal collection of dirty dewdrops*. That put him in his place; he certainly will think twice before playing that trick again'.

'Do you really think so?', the lines sounded a little happier now.

'Oh without a doubt, you'll have a new section plumbed into you before the day's end, and that will be an end of the matter.'

'Well if you put it like that'.

'No other way to look at it...though...'

'Yes?'

'If you could tone down the repartee just a shade we would appreciate it. We nearly cracked our casings laughing so much!'

The turbines good humour was infectious and she saw that there was no need for her to intervene.

Her crew, new and old were becoming a team at last.

And that gave her a good deal of joy.

# GIFTS

Spring, gentle herald of lusty summer lay defeated under a still triumphant winter. Daffodils, ever hopeful struggled under a weight of snow that refused to even look at the calendar, and Pulver was glad that his greatcoat had been designed with the North Atlantic in mind.

Even so he shivered and the owner of the grey-green eyes had shivered even more, despite being fully equipped with coat, scarf and mittens. It was their first journey together and very possibly their last for a long time.

The voice had been grave. 'Take your leave now Mr Pulver. Our orders have changed and you and I, and every man here will be busier than ever.'

Pulver had read the papers and seen the newsreels, he knew just why their orders had changed. The Hood must be ready, and ready soon. So they had journeyed, first to see his family, where his mother had adopted the grey-green eyes as one of her own. He knew the two women would plot and scheme; he knew that his fate was fixed and yet he was content; there were after all worse fates.

And then north, north through ice and cold, past trees fearful of showing so much as a single bud, past streets and houses groaning under a winter's worth of stubborn snow. North to a cottage trembling under the shadows of mountains that wore the snow like a warrior's cloak. North to the man who had placed his feet on a sure path.

North to see the old engineer.

The peat fire did not hiss and roar. Nor did it expend all its energy in showy pyrotechnics. Instead it gave out a steady smouldering heat that defied the outside weather.

They sat around the fire while the old engineer regaled the grey-green eyes with a life time of experiences. Two glasses of the finest malt had loosened a normally reticent tongue and tales of temples and exotic spices were mixed with those of war and death.

And then it was Pulver's turn. The old man interrogated him without mercy for the Hood had been transformed and he had not been there. He had felt the loss and drank up facts and figures in the same way a thirsty plant will gather up welcome rain. He nodded his approval, a lifetime of experience enabling him to visualise every facet of the rebuild.

'Good, Pulver, very good, and how's the old girl taking it?'

Pulver grinned. 'Well enough sir, she complains every now and again.'

The engineer chuckled. 'Aye she would…and so would you young man if we did to you what has been done to her. And I'm about to add to your troubles, though I think you may just thank me before too long.'

He reached out and pulled towards him a plain wooden box and handed it to the grey-green eyes. 'Here lassie, this may just help your young man stay alive.'

She opened the box and pulled out a large green painted bullet.

Her look of puzzlement caused both men to laugh.

'It's only a model ' the old man explained, 'If I brought the real thing in here it may get a wee bit crowded.

A closely typed single sheet of paper had been given to Pulver.

'It's Cardonald's new shell, Mr Pulver.

Pulver nodded expectantly. Cardonald's produced high quality naval shells, and he wondered just how the model had come into the Engineer's hands.

'I do a little consulting work over there', the old man explained, 'and stumbled across them by accident. Some accident of manufacture gives this batch a little more hitting power. Those fools in London refused to see what they had, but I made a phone call and the whole batch is being shipped down this week'. His eyes sparkled with barely suppressed glee. 'When the Hood commissions those shells will be given to her.'

Pulver had quickly scanned the sheet which gave details of the new shell and realised the Hood had been given a gift of which all the other ships would be envious. He recognised the importance of the gift at once.

'Thank you, sir, that's very kind of you. If I'm reading this right, when we fight, anything we hit will really know about it. These shells are better than anything I've seen.'

He had a happy grin on his face which deeply troubled the grey-green eyes. Her rival, the great leviathan that had a piece of his heart, had risen up again like an unwelcome ghost. 'You said *when we fight,* but Mr Chamberlain said there will be no war.' Her eyes became wet with unshed tears. 'And he's wrong isn't he?'

There was a flat sadness in her voice and Pulver and the Engineer exchanged worried glances. Sooner or later this conversation would have had to happen and although he would have wished for a better time and place it looked as if he would have little choice in the matter. There was an almost imperceptible nod from the old man.

It was time.

He took the slim hands in his and gently caressed them hoping to instil some calm into the troubled face.

'There will be war, I don't want there to be one, but I don't get to decide and neither does Mr Chamberlain. There will be war because one man has decided that there will be one. You mustn't worry, I'll be safe, I promise'.

He looked into her only half-convinced face. Could she tell he was lying? Could she know that in war, death's hand was impartial and unseeing?

'You promise?' There was a quavering smile on her face.

He took a deep breath and promised, relieved at the happy smile.

He never realised that she knew he lied.

This was her gift to him. A war unencumbered by any domestic unhappiness. He would fight his war trusting that she had believed him.

This was the life and this was the man she had chosen, but as the old engineer toasted the happy couple she sent a silent prayer winging south to the great ship to keep her man safe.


This was the day.
She'd run.

Every boiler burning.

Every shaft spinning.

She'd turned.

Propellers biting,

Rudder swinging.

This was the day.

Her guns had assaulted the air with smoke and noise.

Hard eyes had looked at her.

Every rivet

Every fleck of paint.

She'd pulled up hard.

Hearts slowing.

Wake dying.

Then she heard the words.

Words that glowed within in her like bright jewels.

The Phoenix flag of Palmer's fluttered in the breeze one last time and then surrendered.

A new flag, long familiar took its place.

Now, at this moment that which was lost was restored.

This was a gift long delayed.

Now she could serve again.

Truly born.

Again.

This was the day.


'Sister?'

The Hood's voice was gentle.

The old ship answered. 'Is it time?'

There was a pause before the Hood replied. This was not an enemy, but a sister, one who served the same cause with the same devotion, so she did her best to be patient and understanding. 'Yes it's time, are you ready?'

There was age in the old ship's reply, age and experience visions of men and places long gone, vanished in time's wake. 'I was young once and so dashing, without care or worry. I remember once I was in a typhoon off Java and I laughed at the joy of it. It was me and my crew against the waves and we won, we won, we won.'

The old voice faltered and died, and the Hood spoke. 'Sister it is time'.

'Will it hurt?'

'No sister I think not, I will be very quick'.

'I was young once.'

'I know.'

'And it won't hurt?'

'No.'

'Then I am ready and happy still to serve...and sister?'

'Yes?'

'Good hunting.'

The Hood's long guns crashed and her sister flew apart and sank almost immediately.

As a trial of her guns and new shells the day was a great success and she returned to the dockside with her crew well pleased.

She was what she was, the Hood reborn.

But that night she cried over a lost sister.


'Too slow! Far too slow!'

The voice from the drone aircraft mocked her and not for the first time. The Hood hated the tiny aircraft that flew with impunity, weaving back and forth, never staying still for long enough, her children annoyed at the taunts from the drone becoming more than they could bear.

Every four point five shell they fired had missed.

Every single one.

Again the mocking laughter lashed at her 'Too slow again, I'll be retired before you even get close. Come on is that the best you can do? Perhaps I should slow down? Is that what you want? Too slow!'

Her children howled in frustration, continuing to fire away to no effect.

This was not practice against static targets, nor even other ships. This was an enemy that moved not in two dimensions, but three.

She could hear the firing computers mumbling arcane figures with increasing frustration, struggling to find a formula that would destroy this impudent intruder. Their instructions to her children became ever more precise, but the insults only ended when the drone flew away, it's voice fading and then falling silent.

It was a chastened ship that returned to port that night, gun barrels cooled, as had tempers. There would be other days and other chances she knew that. But all the same it was very disturbing that just one aircraft was so hard to destroy.

'Christ!'

The voice was soft, almost reverent, but Jack McIntyre knew exactly the emotion that had caused the Leading Seaman to voice his fear. They had burst through the smoke screen intent on getting closer to the Hood than ever before, except this time she was ready.

The great grey shape had begun to blossom with smoke and tiny flowers of brief light, and although each one had nothing more harmful behind it than a small charge it was all too real.

And the Hood got bigger.

And bigger.

'CHRIST!'

This time it was a real oath torn from the man's throat.

The Foxhound had turned hard, very hard indeed, heeling into the sea, the wind howling in protest. Now she ran parallel to the Hood, a little ahead of the battlecruiser. Within seconds of settling on her new course eight pulses of compressed air thrust out a salvo of practice torpedoes and she began her run into the temporary safety of the diminishing smoke cloud.

The Hood had already begun her own high-speed turn, guns still firing seeking to avoid the impudent destroyer's attack. The two ships ended up on the far side of the now vanishing smoke-screen, still running fast through the sea.

A series of flags rose up from the deck of Hood.

'Manoeuvre well executed,' read Jack, proud of his ability to read the flags at such a distance.

The Leading Seaman looked at him with incredulity. 'Well executed? Well fuckin' executed?' The man was now spluttering with outrage. 'You do know Jack that if that had been for real, if that had been a bloody Hun, we would all be in small bloody bits on the bottom of the bloody sea floor.'

Jack thought he knew the answer to that statement.

'Well if that was a Hun then we could have slowed her down enough for one of ours to find her and kill her.'

There was apparently an unanswerable retort for that line of thought.

'A lot of fuckin' good that would do us on the bottom of the sea!'

Jack thought the man had a point, but today had been exciting and wasn't that what life on a destroyer was all about?


It was quiet now. A quarter moon hung low on the restive horizon and both ships moved placidly and slowly through the water.

'You did well today sister'.

The Hood's contralto voice carried far across the water to where the smaller ship was shadowing the battle cruiser.

The reply was instant.

'Thank you sister…it was great fun.'

The Foxhound's voice could not be described as melodious. It skipped from wave to wave in a series of high, hurried barks that like its owner seemed eager to run as fast as they could.

The Hood chuckled at the excited response. 'Yes, my children said the same thing'.

'Your children?'

'My new four point five guns; they had a good deal of fun today and are now sleeping soundly. I hope they did not frighten you, they can be a little…enthusiastic.'

A yelping laugh threw itself against the Hood's grey flanks.

'That they were. My crew were most impressed. And sister, I think we need the practice. I listen to my crew and soon, perhaps very soon, we will paint our bright brass with war paint and darken our deck lights.'

The mood had changed now, the moonlight had somehow chilled the mood and the light-hearted banter had vanished, vanquished by the stern talk of warriors.

'You too have heard then?' The Hood spoke quietly, dampening her excitement.

'War' agreed the Foxhound. 'War close, and war far away. Our enemies gather and threaten sister.'

A dismissive grunt echoed from the Hood. 'I do not fear them. If they gather then they shall be scattered, if they threaten then they will die beneath my guns.'

Despite herself the Foxhound was impressed.

The Hood was not issuing idle boasts but speaking simple and well-known facts and just hearing them made her feel a little more secure.

'But we still practice?' It was not the excitement which now drove the destroyer's question, but the realisation that soon practice would become reality.

'Until war comes,' agreed the Hood. 'Until we are perfect, until none can stand against us.'

'And then?'

The Hood's reply held pride and resignation, honour and expectation. 'I am duty and service. There is no more to say. For me, for you, for all our sisters.'

The Hood was silent now, lost in her thoughts.

But the Foxhound's reply was a low and bloody growl.


The lurid yellow duck took the full force of Churchill's flailing fist and took temporary refuge at the bottom of the bath tub. A wave, laughing at gravity escaped and ran gleefully onto the hardwood floor.

'God damn them all to Hell!'

The duck, believing that the words marked the end of the tempest bobbed happily to the surface and was instantly punished for its presumption.

'Damn them, damn them, damn them all!'

It was childish he knew, and yet strangely satisfying. Months of slights and disappointments blew to the surface in a violent eruption of temper and displaced bath water. Gradually the fists ceased their flailing and the rubber duck cautiously appeared from around the island of his knees and eyed him warily. He gazed back at its smiling face and grimaced sourly. The storm had not gone but was back under carefully forged and well used chains.

This was all so unnecessary. Chamberlain had shuffled his cabinet in response to the Czech crisis, but still there was still no room for Churchill. Even under the threat of war it was obvious that the man still thought that he would disrupt more than he would build.

In his milder moments, moments when the black mood was firmly under control he believed himself to be exceedingly fortunate not to be included in any cabinet, especially now. The dangers, the risks of membership were great and very little would be gained even if the dice had been rolled successfully.

British policy was in a state of chaos.

A worried Paris had dragged London kicking and screaming into supporting their debate at the League of Nations where it was proposed that all of Northern Spain become a mandated territory. The Foreign Office had done their best though to dilute any British support, with the result that once more London appeared muddled and indecisive.

Naturally Spain, Germany and Italy all protested vigorously at the mere thought of any debate. Although having left the League there was little they could directly do, it was still an uncomfortable situation.

And then there was Poland.

Churchill lifted his arm once more at the thought and the duck winced in anticipation. The arm was lowered gently and the duck's plastic smile seemed to shine a little brighter.

German ambitions had once more swung to the east, following their eternal lodestone and once more Paris and London floundered in its wake.

'A country of lions led by jackals' is how Massigli had privately described Poland and he had to agree that only now had Warsaw seen that her forced acquisitions from her neighbours had done nothing but weaken her. Despite that a series of treaties were being formulated that guaranteed not only Poland's borders, but also those of Greece and Rumania. He could only hope that they would be signed and more importantly honoured.

There were few options left now he thought, and none of them were good ones. All the other chances, chances which if grasped would have given peace and security, sunshine and prosperity to millions, had trickled through their fingers un-noticed and un-heeded. All that was left now was to place trip wires around the Axis powers and see which one would start the Conflagration.

And then watch the world burn.

The thought was depressing and once more he felt the black dog struggle against its chains. The duck stirred by some errant current brushed up against him and he looked at it more kindly this time. It had been the undeserved target of much anger and perhaps deserved better of him. He gently pushed the duck under the water and released it. It rose to the surface, triumphant and grinning. Again and again he tried, but the duck was indefatigable. He began to giggle at the fixed smile and bobbing antics of the plastic toy. His black dog of anger howled and pulled at its chains, but it had been defeated by the defiance of the yellow duck.

He giggled again, realising that he and the duck had much in common. He too would arise again; he did not know when, he did not know how but the feeling that had been with him since boyhood; that he had a single destiny, a single purpose comforted him now as it had done in the past.

If the duck could rise despite punishment, despite all that could be thrown at it then so could he.

He would rise again, he was sure of it.

# FAME

The passes were closed. The dead of previous battles guarded them. The dead and the few hundred men that were all Jorge could spare, a few hundred men that mimicked thousands. A scant guard where every man prayed that the memory of past victories would infect the souls of their enemies.

So far his bluff had worked.

Franco and his generals had not thrust men through the narrow winding passes that led to the fertile plains. Instead as he had predicted they had come by sea. Cautiously and with hesitation, for the Asturians and what was left of the Basques had proven they could bite and bite hard. They had landed not in Asturias, nor on the French border, but on their own territory just a few kilometres from the western border of the land that his nation claimed as their own.

It was the very tactic he feared most. Every instinct, every thought told him that to strike at the landing stages instantly was his only hope.

Strike before they could consolidate.

Strike before their courage rose.

Strike before they could take the coast roads.

Strike before it was too late.

He had urged such a campaign, planned and made ready for such a campaign. And been refused. Under no circumstances would their nervous backers in Paris even consider for a moment his army setting so much as a single foot across the border, for fear that such an attempt would re-ignite the Axis powers interest in the Iberian Peninsula.

Jorge had nothing but contempt for such an attitude. He had been fighting Fascism for nearly half a decade and could now barely remember a life before a rifle was thrust into his hand. In his mind a safe Fascist was one that had at least one bullet hole in him and the safest Fascist of all had several holes and no heartbeat. He yearned to make every threatening Fascist as safe as possible.

But he had been refused, and for a day and a night had brooded, thoughts of rebellion, of leading an insurrection against those half brave, half craven men in Gijón to whom he had sworn fealty.

Truly the devil had sat on his shoulder that day. Visions of arrests, of dawn pistol shots, of him as supreme head of all he could see, flooded his mind like a seductive temptress. It took an effort to reject the succubus that had weaved her way into his thoughts, but eventually he realised that while fate had made him a leader of warriors, he would be lost in the dark corridors where politicians navigated like hungry sharks.

Besides had not Spain's own Republican government fallen as much from fratricide as from Fascist bullets? Rebellion now would be to hand Franco the victor's laurels that blood and sacrifice had so far withheld from him.

The very thought had caused him to shiver with fear and distaste and had ended any lingering thoughts of revolt. But if he could not fight the way he wanted, if he could not fight a war where men and guns spoke to each other with blood and fire in pitched battles just how could he fight?

For days he pondered how to fight and how to win.

It was his past that rescued him. His ancestor, the man with the magic gun, the man who had lived and fought submerged in a sea of vicious enemies came to his aid. Had that man not fought and fought courageously with far less means than he had now?

This was the answer he was seeking, the key which would unlock many doors.

He would fight no pitched battles. He would not stand in the open and be slaughtered by a more numerous and better equipped enemy. He would fight as Spaniards had always fought, as his ancestor had fought. He would fade and reform, attack and retire.

This would be his war, the war his men had trained for and relished. He would not force his ragged bands to fight a war they did not know how to fight. Instead he would fight the little war.

A thousand stabs.

A thousand cuts.

A thousand ambushes.

Dead Fascists.

By the score.

By the hundred.

By the thousand.

He smiled as the plans began to form in his head. The bastards wanted to invade his country, his homeland? He would let them come. He would be ready.

Soon there would be many safe Fascists.


They were cowards these communists. Craven abject cowards. Where were they? Not all of them could have been killed in the bombardment. Why would they not stand up like men?

The captain ran with his company up the beach away from the sparkling water, still angry and still puzzled.

They reached the road and deployed with all the skill that long practice had given them.

Still there was nothing. No movement. No resistance. Only unseen birds sang and cried. Only the wind rustled through the tough sea grass.

Silence.

Only silence.

There should have been the shouts of men, the harsh cracks of rifles, and the sharp hiss of hard shrapnel seeking a home in soft flesh.

Nothing. Only the beating of his heart.

Stifling his anger he ordered his men to take the village, hoping that here the Asturians would make a stand.

Nothing.

The village was deserted.

The fishing boats had left. There were no bright white sheets drying in the sun. Even the chickens which adorned the streets of every Spanish village were missing. The white washed walls mocked him, laughed at his anger and his confusion.

He kicked in a door, pistol at the ready. A cool dark interior greeted him, no peasant family lay cowering in the corner.

Nothing.

He began to open drawers and cupboards, his anger growing as he realised that the house had been long since stripped. The last drawer resisted his efforts and with a curse he pulled with all his strength until it shot out with a screech.

It wasn't empty.

It held a short length of fishing line and a short, thin pin. The captain stared at the pin and knew he was dead. His body began to move, but that was instinctive and would never help him.

Three seconds later the armed grenade exploded, showering the captain and his men with deadly slivers of metal and wood.

Jorge's little war had begun.


Ex private, ex corporal, ex sergeant and then ex corporal and lastly once again private.

If Georges Seurat had been prone to melancholy then he would have wept bitter tears over his career in the French army.

But Georges was a fatalist and not at all prone to self-reflection.

He drank. What Frenchmen did not?

He chased and often caught women. Well he was a man and subject to a man's weaknesses.

Unfortunately the Army did not see it that way. In fact they insisted that Georges confine those activities to times when they did not need his services.

Off duty hours in fact.

Not absenting himself from base, remaining sober when he was on duty were apparently rigid rules from which no deviations were allowed.

At last they lost patience with him. He was dismissed from the army and escorted to the gates where two very dubious looking men were waiting for him. They made him a tempting offer, a very tempting offer indeed.

It was a long and tortuous route he had taken, a longer route that the gun that he stood beside had taken he was sure. But it was a gun he knew well. They were old friends who had first met in the dark days after Verdun. He was younger then, a mere boy swept up from the slums of Marseilles to fill savagely depleted ranks. But he knew the Seventy-five, knew it well, knew its kick and its power. Drunk or sober he knew it and could play on it with skill and passion.

But even he had never fired a gun so well hidden. Rocks and brush wood enfolded him, hid him from all but the most knowing of eyes. Only the brazen mouth of the artillery piece poked out of the shelter, looking out blindly across the river.

The hand on his watch swept up to the appointed hour and Georges fired fifteen precisely aimed shells just where they would do the most harm. Even before the last round landed a Renault truck had backed up and willing hands were attaching his gun to the hitching points.

'Move, move, move!'

Georges crew really needed no encouragement, like him they had no wish to be at the receiving end of counter battery fire.

As they drove away into the twilight they heard another gun fire fifteen rounds and then fall silent.

Like them it would live to kill again.


Martha Gellhorn's feet ached and were bleeding. Sweat stung her eyes and carved delicate tracks through the dust on her face. She longed for a brush or even a comb, and a bath would be akin to heaven. But ultimately she was happy to forgo them knowing that they were not important. All she cared about was this interview, the last and hopefully the greatest.

She'd interviewed them all.

Her note pad and pen had recorded men who spoke of destiny while sheltering in cellars against the incessant bombing.

She'd photographed women queueing for food, patient and weary.

She'd talked to teachers, teaching without books and doctors healing without medicine.

She'd wandered through battle fields where the ground grew fresh corpses and echoed to whimpers and screams.

Her camera recorded abandoned farmhouses, burning villages and the faces of men and women swinging at the end of ropes.

Everywhere there was a stoic courage a calmness which impressed her far more than any rousing speech.

Not a nation at war, but a people.

Still she wandered, notebook ever in her hands.

She'd talked with his lieutenants.

El Platero, the former silversmith whose mounted rifles stung and vanished only to reform and kill again. Alvaraze, the poet, master both of artillery and rhyme, whose hands perpetually gripped a book of verse. And then there was Hugh O'Neill.

O'Neill the charming and oh so dangerous man, who claimed that the blood of Irish kings ran in his veins. If it did it ran cold, very cold indeed. The man took a savage delight in torture, and death was a merciful release for any Fascist who fell into his hands. Of course that death came only after every scrap of information had been surrendered.

Of all that she interviewed he alone failed to raise any other emotion other than plain fear. Yet she did not show that fear, for she recognised that to do so would put her in mortal danger. Men such as O'Neill fed on fear, needed it in fact in the same way as they needed air or water. So she smiled warmly, armoured against his charm, knowing that her American passport and safe conduct would avail her little if the courteous man with the carefully clipped moustache decided to pounce.

Perhaps it was his vanity, perhaps it was curiosity, but whatever it was at last he agreed to give her a guide to see the man who all Europe had begun to notice, but who remained an enigma.

Who was the man who defeated the Fascists in the passes which led through the Cantabrian mountains? Where had he come from, and did he really think that his campaign of mass guerrilla warfare would defeat forces that had utterly defeated the Republican forces? Who was he, the man that even the Spanish people had been unable to give a nickname to? The man known simply as Jorge.

There was a world outside of Spain. Jorge knew this. After all there were volunteers in his army from France, from America, from England, even from Italy and Germany. Yes there was a world outside the mountains and beyond the sea, but the thought that the world would wish to know about him had never entered his head.

But the strange American had insisted, had endured much to see him, and oddly enough had seemed satisfied with his answers.

What could he tell her? She teased the answers out of him, each one leading to the next. She assured him that he would, through her words become famous, and seemed genuinely upset when he laughed in her face.

Yes a very strange woman and a very strange day, but it was over now and he had a war to wage and a list of very tempting targets.

He forgot about the woman and began to think about a poorly supported Fascist brigade some distance away.

It was time to make these particular Fascist pay the price of invasion.

Soon he would add them to the list of Fascists made safe.


'Fame? What do I need fame for?'

His words had shaken her more than a little. His laughter was not harsh or mocking but born out of genuine puzzlement mixed with a little embarrassment.

'I have all that I wish, brave men and women surround me, I have an enemy to defeat and a land to protect.' The laughter had ended with a grinning shake of his head. 'I have no need for fame, Miss Gelhorn. I am just a simple peasant and peasants do no more than live and die.'

She had tried to convince Jorge, but he either could not, or would not see that that fame had indeed come to him. But she had him now, his history, his motivations, his very life and the life of his people. As she walked away from his camp she was already formulating the book that would be born out all she had seen.

The title was of course obvious. She believed that 'No Need For Fame' was going to be a very important book indeed.


She would not be afraid.

Her friend the doll was not afraid, and her mother was not afraid so she was determined not to be.

Though she thought of herself as a young lady, she was still too young to realise that her mother's smile was just as artificial as the smile painted on the doll that she firmly gripped to her chest.

Her father had left with the others, rifle clumsily slung over his shoulder. She remembered being swung up in the air and lifted to his face for a last kiss. She remembered his beard, the scent of rough tobacco, his sad eyes, his hair in need of cutting. She remembered her mother straightening his ill-made uniform, hands busy lest her eyes weep more tears.

She would not be afraid.

They sang songs in the cellar.

While the bombs fell.

While Gijón burned.

Happy songs, funny songs, songs of resistance and rebirth.

Her friend was not afraid and comforted her. She had less hair now, and her dress was faded and tattered, but her smile was as bright as ever.

She helped her mother and the other women prepare the food, and when it was ready she took the plates to the old and the infirm with the grave and delicate courtesy that her mother had taught her. They were not afraid and thanked her with equally bright smiles.

She sat in the corner, plate wiped clean and told her doll that she was not afraid. The doll smiled back at her. Matching its courage with hers.

The cellar shook.

But they were not afraid.

# RIGHT WILL PREVAIL

David Riley picked up the single sheet of paper. Even as mayor of Jarrow he did not have this kind of paper. It was heavily embossed and in his opinion far too ornate and far too expensive.

Needless frippery he had described it to Ellen Wilkinson who had merely grinned and pointed out that such symbols were entirely necessary in the world he was moving into.

'You and I David,' she had said, '…know better but there are those who believe in such things and take comfort from them.'

She'd laughed at his grimace. 'Oh yes David there are even those who will be impressed by this sort of thing. But we've done well David, you and I and the people. We've taken a dying town and breathed new life into it, put the light back into many an eye and food on many a table. And we've built this, all of this on the back of a broken ship. So don't complain David, you've earned this. We all have.'

And then she'd left, back to London, back to an increasingly anxious Parliament, though promising to come back soon.

He stared again at the paper running his finger over the raised letters, his hand reading the words as much as his eyes; *The Confederation of British Ship Repairers.*

Jarrow might never build another ship again but had proved that she could rebuild better than new. It was all that Palmer's new owners needed, proof that their gamble had paid off.

The launching of the Hood had been the launching of a new idea.

Every Mayor, ever councilman, from every town that had contributed to the rebuild had attended.

It was, though they did not realise it a powerful group.

John Sumner represented the steel mill owners, the true controllers of Palmer's Shipyard and he had waited until the last sandwich had been eaten and the last bottle had been drained dry. And then he spoke. He spoke not of lofty ideals or great humanitarian causes, but of Pounds, Shillings and Pence. He spoke of profits, not for him alone, but for all.

He reminded his guests that Jarrow had spread money and jobs far and wide, jobs that had votes behind them. He reminded them that the Hood would leave soon and those jobs and more importantly those votes would leave with her. He asked that they support him in gaining more work for Jarrow and for the two smaller firms that the steel makers had bought. They were all holders of government bonds that provided the money to rebuild the Hood and he would not ask for more money, but he would ask that they use their influence to lobby for him.

The few MP's that had attended looked a little uncomfortable at that suggestion but David knew from his own experience that it was a foolish MP that ignored his town's council, whatever their political differences.

It was a shrewd move by Sumner and the men he represented. Now if all went well they had acquired more political influence than ever before. And not just political influence at Westminster; several union leaders had attended the launch and he had noticed with interest John Summers and Palmer's managers deep in conversation with them. It was not a deep conversation but looked more as if they were confirming something already agreed on.

He tried to move through the crowd, his curiosity aroused, but at every step there was a hand to shake or a few words to say and the strange meeting, if it was a meeting, broke up long before he could reach it.

He never did find out that afternoon just what was happening, but later that evening when he met John Sumner and Ellen Wilkinson all his questions were answered. It was what he had hoped for and campaigned for, the only question being just how could he find the time to do two jobs?

'But your good shirt is not ironed and my new dress needs washing'.

It was typical Geordie thought that Mabel would think of such things at a time like this. He had been married long enough now though to keep such thoughts to himself and watched a half-demented wife run around his house tidying the already tidy and dusting the already dusted.

'The step', she wailed 'I haven't cleaned the step'.

A pail of hot water was immediately procured and Mabel rushed out, probably with the intention of cleaning not only the step, but the surrounding pavement.

He resisted the laugh that was trying to escape. It would not help, and if he did succumb, Mabel would make him suffer far in excess of what a momentary weakness was worth.

He glanced at the short note that had been delivered by the morning mail. Miss Ellen Wilkinson and guest the note had said, giving a time only a few hours away.

He grunted, Mabel might panic, fearful that her domestic skills would be called into question, but he had learnt never to panic, only to question.

He had hoped after the Hood was launched that he could descend into a life of obscurity, a few shillings in his pocket, a quiet pint or two with the lads, his horizons now after all his adventures shrinking back to comfortable normality. So what did Wilkinson want and who was her guest?

There was no point in worrying and later he was able to greet his guests with a calmness that did much to counter Mabel's agitation.

She needn't have worried, Wilkinson was charming, complimenting Mabel on her house, pointing out to her guest the photographs of Jack in his uniform and Geordie handing over his clock to a now exiled Prince of Wales.

It was the guest that intrigued Geordie. The name meant nothing to him though Wilkinson explained that John Sumner represented the steel makers, the true owners of Palmer's.

Though the man was unfamiliar he was no stranger to the type. He'd noticed the man looking over and through him as he sipped tea from Mabel's favourite cup. It was the look he'd seen a thousand times in the trenches. It was the look a seasoned colonel gave a new second lieutenant. The man was judging him, measuring him and taking his time doing so.

This was obviously a man used to making difficult decisions, but only after considering every factor.

Geordie felt no impatience. The man was polite enough or shrewd enough to visit Geordie in his own home and he could wait while his wife and Wilkinson chattered away.

Summers put his cup down with a casual deliberation which Geordie could only admire. There was a fluidity in the motion, not a single action wasted. As he had guessed the man was in control of every aspect of his life; indeed would feel uncomfortable if he wasn't.

He shifted in his chair as he noticed a silent interchange between the man and Wilkinson.

'Geordie', she began 'I've been telling Mr Summers about you, how you marched for us, how you never gave up.'

Summers took off his glasses in what was obviously a habitual gesture, polished them and placed them back on his head, never for one moment taking his eyes off Geordie. 'That's was a great thing you did Mr. McIntyre and one I can admire. I can't say we'll ever agree about politics but you saw what needed to be done and you did it.'

Geordie was about to explain that his wife and Wilkinson were the real drivers behind his march, but a warning glance from Mabel killed the thought before it could be born as words and he let the industrialist continue.

'Times are changing Mr McIntyre, changing fast and if we don't change with them then then I fear that we will not survive; that Jarrow will not survive. But I can't do it alone. I've been talking to people, Miss Wilkinson, the leaders of your own union, many, many people. I've told them what I've seen in America, and what I've done at my own steelworks. I've seen new methods, new tooling, new ways of working with people. There was resistance, I'll be honest, from the unions and from my management. I was accused of being mad, and worse I was accused of being a communist'.

He laughed dryly.

'I may be mad Mr McIntyre, but I assure you that I've never voted anything but Conservative. What I am is a businessman. I see a problem and come up with a solution. Mr McIntyre, you are an exceptional man and I want you to be part of that solution.'

Geordie remained puzzled. He didn't consider himself exceptional. As a man he had done what needed to be done to protect his family, but nothing more than that. He did not have the reply that he knew the man was waiting for and the conversation died.

It was Wilkinson who broke the silence, sensing Geordie's reluctance and reticence.

'Geordie, Palmer's has a new contract, an auxiliary cruiser, you know that?'

Geordie nodded, the news had come as a great relief.

'Well Geordie what you do not know is that the cruiser is an experiment in Mr Sumner's new methods.'

'A single ship' interrupted Sumner and yes an experiment with no promises on either side, not on mine, nor by the unions. I think that it will succeed and benefit all, but there's bound to be rough spots, and that is where you come in. I need an umpire, someone who is not afraid to take on difficult tasks, someone who has the respect of management and unions, a man who can see practical solutions where others can see only ingrained problems, someone who can put out fires on the shop floor before they become unmanageable.

'Oh you won't be alone. Other people, your own mayor amongst them will cover other areas but on the shop floor your word will count for a good deal.

'I'm not a bad judge of character Mr McIntyre; your record alone would recommend you and I think that you are capable of carrying out all that is required.'

He paused and again took of his glasses and began polishing them waiting for Geordie to reply. The glasses were returned to Sumner's head and the man looked questioningly at Geordie, who could see his quiet life vanishing down a long dark tunnel. He looked around seeing Wilkinson smiling encouragingly and then his wife who was looking at Sumner's, judging the steel maker in the same way Sumner had judged Geordie.

The silence stretched and stretched with no one able to break it.

Finally Mabel finished her assessment, and Geordie feared that his life was about to change again.

He was right.

'You'll need to get your suit pressed Geordie', she said simply.


'Rather a good show this chap's doing.'

Keyes pointed to the photograph that accompanied Gellhorn's article, knowing that Churchill would rise to the bait like a hungry trout.

A hand reached out through the cigar smoke and grasped the newspaper. A brandy flavoured and dismissive grunt was issued as Churchill looked at a photograph of Jorge resplendent in his sheepskin coat and binoculars.

'Bolsheviks.'

The one word summed up a lifetime attitude and was exactly the response that Keyes expected and though he too had no great love for any of Marx's disciples he felt that his friend was too rigid in his opinion. Keyes reclaimed the paper and tapped at the article.

'Gelhorn says not,' he said. She says that Gijón has broken with Moscow and promised to introduce moderate policies, socialist of course, but still moderate. And they are doing well Winston, Bolsheviks or not. The whole country in in arms, Franco's having a hard time of it, that much is certain'.

A second grunt was issued, even more dismissive than the first. 'They broke with Moscow did they, or did Moscow break with them? Still they do seem to have adopted some of the tactics I saw in South Africa, but whether they can win, whether the French will continue to supply them are questions only time can answer.'

'Certainly having France as a main sponsor has forced them, at least on the surface to radically change their political outlook.'

'But to my mind the French are playing with fire, what if Franco gets German backing once more, what then? Not that this in any way helps us here, and it certainly doesn't help the Prime Minister with his wish to build stronger ties with the Russians. There are some very strange tales floating about these days, tales of secret meetings, of a possible treaty or a least some sort of agreement between Berlin and Moscow.'

Now it was Keynes turn to be dismissive. He drew deeply on his cigarette and added its fumes to the Havana smoke that his friend had contributed to the room. 'An agreement between Hitler and Stalin? After all they've said about each other? Not a chance, Winston. You mark my words, Stalin will recognise that his best allies are us and the French. We'll have a treaty with them long before the year's out, and then the Germans will be neatly boxed in. And that,' he said decisively, '…will be the end of Hitler'.

An anticipatory grin appeared on his face. 'Gone by Christmas I imagine'.

Churchill took a reflective sip of brandy and shook his head. 'But what if I'm right, Keyes. What if my sources are correct and our government and the French are unable to convince Moscow? What if our Prime Minister is powerless to convince Stalin that his best interests lie with us, that we do indeed have a common enemy, what then? What if Stalin sees, as he must see, that any involvement with the security of Poland would mean the Red Army marching to the aid of the Poles? Why would he do that, what would he gain, other than a war where he would do all the bleeding?' An ironical laugh escaped Churchill's cherubic face.

'After all in the event of war over Poland what would be our contribution? It's not as if we could sail a battleship down the main street of Warsaw now is it?'

Keyes smiled at the thought. 'That would be a sight to see, but I still think I'm right. The Russians will join us, maybe not for ever, but long enough to see Hitler toppled. I'm certain that now we've made a stand Germany will be forced to pull back, and haven't you always said that once dictators are confronted their end is not far away?

'Gone by Christmas,' he repeated.

Churchill did not reply. An awful sense of foreboding enveloped him and instincts long honed told him that his friend was wrong, very wrong.

No treaty could save the world now. It was already too late.

Far too late.


Chamberlains final words were full of constrained sadness 'And against them I am certain that the right will prevail'.

Mabel's hand lay inside his, cool and damp. They listened as the calm, unhurried voice of the BBC announcer told the nation the new regulations under which they now lived. Though he did not know it for one room in one house in Jarrow his words were wasted, they were neither heard nor acknowledged. Only her hand was truly part of her right now, and through that hand her husband, her friend, her lover, the father of her children. She felt his hand tighten on hers and his words telling her that all would be well and that he would be beside her always.

It was comforting to know that now, as always she wasn't alone. She had her family and her home. And she was determined that nothing would take that away from her.

She would keep her family safe.

Always.

Come what may.


'And against them I am certain that the right will prevail'.

She'd been warned, but still the grey-green eyes wept bitter tears that tracked down her face and joined in a tiny cascade at the very edge of her chin. The man who loved her was not at her side, and what was worse was even now with her rival, a rival who would take him not into safety but deliberately and with malice straight into the path of danger. And yet it was where he needed to be, and that would the price she would pay if she wished to become his wife.

She picked up the framed photograph of their last time together. How handsome he looked in his uniform, the single ring of his rank standing out plainly against the dark almost black jacket. And yet only a few days later her great, grey rival had swallowed him and put immeasurable distance between them. And now as she had feared, as he had predicted, there was war.

She looked at his half shy, half wry smile and an answering smile began to form on her face, and though she longed for him she thought of his last letter. She read again the carefully crafted pages, written so neatly in the purple ink that he had adopted from the old engineer.

They were words of love and encouragement, of caution and warning. She could hear his voice in the words and feel his touch. The tears hesitated and stopped, the last of them vanquished by a hastily drawn handkerchief long before it could follow the path its brothers had forged.

She would not cry, there would be no more sadness.

Whatever the future brought, whether it was good tidings or ill she would face it as if he were always by her side.

She would make him proud, she would be worthy of him.

Come what may.


'And against them I am certain that the right will prevail'.

She watched her husband rise and gently turn off the radio and walk to the window and look over gardens where summer still held sway. Nearly thirty years of marriage, of times good and bad had taught her that this was a time for silence. Many long minutes fled into the irretrievable past before he moved and spoke.

'Poor Neville, did you hear him?'

'A bitter blow. How hard he must be taking it. He tried so hard. Never has a man run so hard, with so much ardour down the wrong road. Poor, poor Neville'. He shook his head and she knew that he was genuinely upset over the pain the Prime Minister had felt.

She too had heard the restrained grief and anger that coloured Chamberlain's speech. She knew her husband well and felt pride that today of all days he had elected to be here with her, even if it was for a few brief hours. It was a devotion decades in the making, but she knew better than to presume on it.

She touched his shoulder. 'You must go Winston, they will need you'.

He nodded, sadness fighting with excitement in an unsuccessful struggle across the battle ground that was his face.

She watched the car drive away, taking her husband to what he believed to be his long-awaited destiny.

And watched dry eyed. There were no tears, for how could she rage against fate?

He was her husband, her Winston, but that was only a small facet of the man. There were other larger facets and she knew that soon they would flash into life. But she would continue as she had always done.

She would be wherever he was.

Come what may.


The Tannoy's background hum ended with a harsh click and they were left alone with the captain's words still echoing from the steel walls.

It was war.

They knew it was coming, everyone, no matter what his rank, had known it was coming but to hear the words caused each one of them for a moment to retreat behind the inner wall that every man carried as his ultimate defence.

War, stark and uncompromising had come.

It was Stebbings who broke the silence. 'Bastards have asked for it'.

Stebbings was a man of few words and most of them were profane, but his voice was calm almost flat. It was almost Pulver thought as if he was discussing the most trivial of events. He looked again, but Stebbings face remained calm, almost impassive.

There was a low rumble of agreement from the men, glad that their thoughts had found a voice. They too had long since come to terms with the new reality just as he had.

A very faint smile broke Stebbings calm exterior as he looked at his lieutenant. 'Good news for you though, sir'.

Pulver was puzzled and looked up in surprise.

He looked at the now grinning seaman but could detect no malice, so he put a note of mock sarcasm in his voice. 'And how Stebbings does the outbreak of war in any way aid me?'

Now it was Stebbings turn to look puzzled. 'Well sir you're bound to get your second ring up now, aren't you?'

There was a burst of laughter which did much to break the tension Pulver had not thought of war in terms of promotion, but the ever practical Stebbings had.

The laughter died away and the day continued. War or no war the life of the Hood went on; there were jobs to do, tasks to complete.

The Hood's routine would remain the same.

They would do their duty.

Come what may.


'Vive le peuple français! Vive la France!'

With those last words Leon Blum stood as the Marseillaise sang its song of glory and resistance to tyranny. He hoped it was a good omen. He drew a deep breath as the studio once more burst into noisy and bright life. All over France his words would be heard and even now telegrams would be chattering down the lines to every corner of France over the water. From the languid lagoons of the Pacific to the tangled jungles of Asia his voice would be heard.

France, his France had declared war on Germany, and for the second time in his life Gaul and Teuton would dance to the beat of death's drum.

He wasn't needed here now, and the looks of pity and sorrow were more than he could bear. There was a car waiting and he got in it and drove away through the half-deserted streets. He had tried to avert war, with all his skill, with all his power.

And he had failed.

There were no more rabbits he could pull out of his hat.

Now there were only swords.


There was Wagner on the Radio and that was always a bad sign.

Georg Maikranz relished his Sundays. They were a day for church, and for a few bottles of beer.

And relaxation.

That, if he were honest, above all.

His wife would be shocked at that thought. For her Sunday was church day, a day when she prayed for her family, but mercifully she was shielded from the pressure of the shipyard. And that pressure had risen from an already high level and even he with all his strength and love of order had struggled to cope.

The situation in Poland had not helped, with ever more frantic and impossible directives being directed at him and his staff. He disliked panic and disorder and this looked very much like both, but he hoped that soon when this business in the east was over some sense of normality would return.

He took a meditative swallow of beer and listened as the music faded and the voice announced that Germany was once more at war.

He watched his wife slump in her chair and he knew at once where her thoughts had flown. To their only son, assigned to the Bismarck.

He sternly repressed his own memories of blood and mud, of comrades easily made and easily lost and ran to his wife. Only she mattered for the moment. He must comfort her, divert her thoughts along better, happier paths. So he told her that her son was on a ship that was not ready for war, would not, could not be used. He told her that the war would be long over before the Bismarck could fire her guns in anger. Over and over he told her until a last a small smile broke through and she was reassured.

Only his thoughts now remained and they must never be revealed to her. He remembered fighting the British and how stubborn and unyielding they could be.

And one memory above all bit and cut at him.

He remembered marching to the front in 1914, believing that by Christmas he would back home.

And that memory refused to die.

The story continues in 'An Extra Knot Part II'

# FICTION FROM APS BOOKS

(www.andrewsparke.com)

Davey J Ashfield *Contracting With The Devil*
HR Beasley: *Nothing Left To Hide*
Lee Benson: *So You Want To Own An Art Gallery*
Lee Benson: *Where's Your Art gallery Now?*
Nargis Darby: *A Different Shade Of Love*
Jean Harvey: *Pandemic*
Michel Henri: *Mister Penny Whistle*
Michel Henri: *The Death Of The Duchess Of Grasmere*
Michel Henri: *Abducted By Faerie*
Hugh Lupus *An Extra Knot*
Ian Meacheam: *An Inspector Called*
Tony Rowland: *Traitor Lodger German Spy*
Andrew Sparke: *Abuse Cocaine & Soft Furnishings*
Andrew Sparke: *Copper Trance & Motorways*
Phil Thompson: *Momentary Lapses In Concentration*
Paul C. Walsh: *A Place Between The Mountains*
Michael White: *A Life Unfinished*

44213381R00102

Made in the USA
Middletown, DE
04 May 2019